"Perfectly understandable, Princess. You have been through a testing time."

Aisha nodded and gave a matter-of-fact smile, relieved she hadn't plunged their two countries into some kind of diplomatic crisis. After all, she was being offered protection here in a neighboring country. Sanctuary. She should not abuse that courtesy. "Then I will not waste any more of your time, Sheikh Zoltan. I will wait in my suite until my father arrives."

He took her hand and she felt a sizzle of recognition, of having held a hand like this one before—a hand that belonged to a man who ran with long, powerful strides…

Impossible!

"Tell me one thing," she said, disturbed enough to remember another niggling question that had not been answered. "Why did my father send all of my belongings here when I will be in Al-Jirad such a short time? Surely he must have realized I could have made do with a suitcase full at the most? Why do you think he did that?"

He shrugged, her hand still wrapped securely in his. "Maybe he thought you would need them afterwards."

"Afterwards? After what?"

"After we are married, of course."

Trish Morey

DUTY AND THE BEAST

HARLEQUIN®
entertain, enrich, inspire™

Recycling programs
for this product may
not exist in your area.

ISBN-13: 978-0-373-13093-1

DUTY AND THE BEAST

Copyright © 2012 by Trish Morey

This edition published by arrangement with Harlequin Books S.A.

For questions and comments about the quality of this book,
please contact us at CustomerService@Harlequin.com.

® and TM are trademarks of Harlequin Enterprises Limited or its
corporate affiliates. Trademarks indicated with ® are registered in the
United States Patent and Trademark Office, the Canadian Trade Marks
Office and in other countries.

www.Harlequin.com

Printed in U.S.A.

All about the author...
Trish Morey

TRISH MOREY wrote her first book at age 11 for a children's book-week competition. Entitled *Island Dreamer*, it told the story of an orphaned girl and her life on a small island at the mouth of South Australia's Murray River. *Island Dreamer* also proved to be her first rejection—her entry was disqualified unread and, shattered and broken, she turned to a life where she could combine her love of fiction with her need for creativity—Trish became a chartered accountant! Life wasn't all dull though, as she embarked on a skydiving course, completing three jumps before deciding that she'd given her fear of heights a run for its money.

Meanwhile, she fell in love and married a handsome guy who cut computer code, and Trish penned her second book—the totally riveting *A Guide to Departmental Budgeting*—whilst working for the NZ Treasury.

Back home in Australia after the birth of their second daughter, Trish spied an article saying that Harlequin Books was actively seeking new authors. It was one of those "Eureka!" moments—Trish was going to be one of those authors!

Eleven years after reading that fateful article (actually June 18th, 2003, at 6:32 p.m!) the magical phone call came and Trish finally realized her dream.

According to Trish, writing and selling a book is a major life achievement that ranks up there with jumping out of an airplane and motherhood. All three take commitment, determination and sheer guts, but the effort is so very, very worthwhile.

Trish now lives with her husband and four young daughters in a special part of South Australia, surrounded by orchards and bushland and visited by the occasional koala and kangaroo.

You can visit Trish at her website at www.trishmorey.com or drop her a line at trish@trishmorey.com.

Other titles by Trish Morey available in eBooks

Harlequin Presents®

CHAPTER ONE

THEY came for her in the dead of night, while the camp was silent but for the rustle of palm leaves on the cool night air and the snort of camels dreaming of desert caravans long since travelled. She was not afraid when she heard the zip of the blade through the wall of the tent. She was not even afraid when a man dressed all in black, his face covered by a mask tied behind his head and with only slits for his eyes, stepped inside, even though his height and the width of his shoulders were enough to steal her breath away and cause her pulse to trip.

Instead it was relief that flooded her veins and brought her close to tears, relief that the rescue she had prayed and hoped so desperately for had finally arrived.

'I know you would come for me,' she whispered as she slid fully dressed out of bed to meet him, almost tripping over her slippers in her rush to get away. She swallowed back a sob, knowing what she was escaping, knowing how close she had come. But at last she would be safe. There was no need to be afraid.

But when the hand clamped hard over her mouth to silence her, and she felt herself pulled roughly against his hard, muscular body, there was no denying her sudden jag of fear.

'Do not utter another word, Princess,' the man hissed into her ear as he dipped his head to hers. 'Or it may be your last.'

She stiffened even as she accepted the indignity, for she had been raised to accept no stranger's touch. But she had little choice now, with his arm like a steel band around her waist, the fingers of one large hand splayed from her chest to her belly and the palm of his other hand plastered hard across her mouth so that she could all but taste his heated flesh.

Unnecessarily close.

Unnecessarily possessive.

Every breath she took contained his scent, a blend of horseflesh and leather, of shifting sands and desert air, all laced with a warm, musky scent that wormed its way into all the places he touched her and beyond. Those places burned with heat until unnecessarily possessive became unnecessarily intimate, and some innate sense of survival pounded out a message in her heartbeat, warning her that perhaps she was not as safe as she had supposed.

Something inside her rebelled. Foolish man! He might be here to rescue her but hadn't she been ready and waiting? Did he imagine she had prayed for rescue only to scream or run and risk her chances of escape?

She was sick of being manhandled and treated like a prize, first by Mustafa's goons and now by her own father's. She was a princess of Jemeya, after all. How dared this man handle her like some common sack of melons he might have picked up at the market?

He shifted and she squirmed, hoping to take advantage of his sudden stillness while his focus seemed elsewhere, but there was no escape. The iron band simply pulled her tighter against the hard wall of his body, his fingers tightening on her flesh, punching the air from her lungs. She gasped, her lips parting, and felt one long finger intrude between her lips.

Shock turned to panic as she tasted his flesh in her mouth.

She felt invaded. She felt violated with the intimacy of the act.

So she did the only possible thing she could. She bit down.

Hard.

He jumped and spat out a curse under his breath, but, while he shifted his fingers away from the danger of her teeth, he did not let her go. 'Be still!' he hissed, holding her tighter, even closer to his rigid form, so that she was convinced he must be made of rock. Warm, solid rock but with a drum beating at its core. Once more she was reminded that this man was not just some nameless rescuer, not just a warrior sent by her father, but a man of flesh and blood, a beating heart and a hot hand that touched her in places no man's hand had a right to be. A hand that stirred a strange pooling heat deep in her belly...

She was glad she had bitten him. She hoped it hurt like hell. She would gladly tell him that too, if only he would take his damned hand off her mouth.

And then she heard it—a short grunt from outside the tent—and she froze as the curtains twitched open.

Ahmed, she realised as the unconscious guard was flopped to the carpet by a second bandit clad similarly in black. Ahmed, who had leered hungrily at her every time he had brought in her meals, laughing at her when she had insisted on being returned to her father, telling her with unrestrained glee exactly what Mustafa planned on doing with his intended bride the moment they were married.

The bandit's eyes barely lingered on her before he nodded to the man at her back. 'Clear for now, but go quickly. There are more.'

'And Kadar?'

'Preparing one of his "surprises".'

All at once she was moving, propelled by her nameless rescuer towards the slash in the tent wall, her slippered feet barely grazing the carpeted floor. He hesitated there just a fraction, testing the air, listening intently, before he set her down, finally loosening his grip but not nearly enough to excise the blistering memory of his large hand spreading wide over her belly.

'Can you run as hard as you bite?' he asked quietly, his voice husky and low as he wrapped his large hand around hers, scanning the area one last time before he looked down at her.

The glinting light in his eyes made her angrier than ever. Now he was laughing at her? She threw him an icy look designed to extinguish any trace of amusement. 'I bite harder.'

Even in the dark she thought she sensed the scarf over his mouth twitch before a cry rang out across the camp behind them.

'Let's hope you're wrong,' he muttered darkly, tugging her roughly into a run beside him, his hand squeezing hers with a grip of steel, the second man guarding their rear as together they scaled the low dune, shouts of panic and accusation now building behind them.

Adrenaline fuelled her lungs and legs—adrenaline and the tantalising thought that as soon as they were safe she was going to set her father's arrogant mercenary right about how to treat a princess.

From the camp behind came an order to stop, followed by the crack of rifle fire and a whistle as the bullet zinged somewhere over their heads, and she soon forgot about being angry with her rescuer. They would not shoot her, she reasoned. They would not dare harm a princess of Jemeya and risk sparking an international incident. But it was dark and her captors were panicking and she had no intention of testing her theory.

Neither had she any intention of complying with the command to stop, even if the man by her side had any hint of letting her go. No way would she let herself be recaptured, not when Mustafa's ugly threats still made her shudder with revulsion. Marry a slug like Mustafa? No way. This was the twenty-first century. She wasn't going to be forced into marrying anybody.

So she clung harder to her rescuer's hand and forced her feet to move faster across the sand, her satin slippers cracking through the dune's fragile crust until, heavy and dragging with sand, her foot slipped from one and she hesitated momentarily when he jerked her forwards.

'Leave it,' he snapped, urging her on as another order to stop and another shot rang out, and she let the other slipper be taken by the dune too, finding it easier to keep up with him barefoot as they forged across the sand. Her lungs and muscles burned by the time they had scaled the dune and plunged over the other side, her mouth as dry as the ground beneath her bare feet. As much as she wanted to flee, as much as she had to keep going or Mustafa's men would surely hunt her down, she knew she could not keep going like this for long.

Over the sound of her own ragged breath she heard it—a whistle piercing the sky, and then another, until the night sky became a screaming promise that ended with a series of explosions bursting colour and light into the dark night. The cries from behind them became more frantic and panicked and all around was the acrid smell of gunpowder.

'What did you do to them?' she demanded, feeling suddenly sickened as the air above the camp glowed now with the flicker of flame from burning tents. Escape was one thing, but leaving a trail of bloodied and injured—maybe even worse—was another.

He shrugged as if it didn't matter, and she wanted to pull her hand free and strike him for being so callous.

'You did want to be rescued, Princess?' Then he turned, and in the glow from the fires she could make out the dark shape of someone waiting for them, could hear the low nicker of the horses he held. Four horses, one for each of them, she noted, momentarily regretting the loss of her shoes until she realised all she would be gaining. She didn't care if her feet froze in the chill night air or rubbed raw on the stirrups. It was a small price to pay for some welcome space from this man. How she could do with some space from him.

'Surely,' she said, as they strode towards the waiting horses, 'you didn't have to go that far?'

'You don't think you're worth it?' Once again she got the distinct impression he was laughing at her. She looked away in sheer frustration, trying to focus on the positives. Her father had sent rescuers. Soon she would see him again. And soon she would be in her own home, where people took her seriously, and where men didn't come with glinting eyes, hidden smiles and hands that set off electric shocks under her skin.

She could hardly wait.

She was already reaching for the reins of the closest horse when his hand stopped her wrist. 'No, Princess.'

'No? Then which one's mine?'

'You ride with me.'

'But there are four...'

'And there are five of us.'

'But...' And then she saw them, two more men in black running low across the dunes towards them when she had been expecting only one.

'Kadar,' he said, slapping one of the men on the back as they neared, making her wonder how he could tell which one was which when they looked indistinguishable to her. 'I'm afraid the princess didn't think much of your fireworks.'

Fireworks? she thought as the man called Kadar feigned disappointment, her temper rising. They were only *fireworks*?

'Apologies, Princess,' the one called Kadar said with a bow. 'Next time I promise to do better.'

'They served their purpose, Kadar. Now let's go before they remember what they were doing before the heavens exploded.'

She looked longingly at the horse she had chosen, now bearing the man who'd been waiting for them in the dunes. A man who, like the others, was tall and broad and powerfully built.

Warriors, she guessed as they swung themselves with ease onto their mounts. Mercenaries hired by her father to rescue her. Maybe he had spent his money wisely, maybe they were good at what they did, but still, she couldn't wait to see the back of them.

Especially the one who took liberties with his hands and with his tongue.

'Are you ready, Princess?' he asked, and before she had time to snap a response she found herself lifted bodily by the waist onto the back of the last remaining horse, her impossible rescuer launching himself behind and tucking her in close between him and the reins, before wrapping a cloak around them both until she was bundled up as if she was in a cocoon.

'Do you mind?' she said, squirming to put some distance between them.

'Not at all,' he said, tugging the cloak tighter and her closer with it, setting the horse into motion across the sand. 'We have a long way to go. You will find it easier if you relax.'

Not a chance.

'You could have told me,' she said, sitting as stiffly as she could in front of him, pretending that there was a chasm between them instead of a mere few thin layers of fabric. She tried to ignore the arm at her back cradling her and wished away the heat that flared in every place where their bodies rocked together with the motion of the horse.

'Could have told you what?'

'That they were only fireworks.'

'Would you have believed me?'

'You let me think it was much worse.'

'You think too much.'

'You don't know the first thing about me.'

'I know you talk too much.' He hauled her even closer to him. 'Relax.'

She yawned. 'And you're arrogant and bossy.'

'Go to sleep.'

But she didn't want to go to sleep. If she went to sleep, she would slump against him, closer to that hard wall of his chest, closer to that beating heart. And princesses did not fall asleep on the chests of strangers mounted on horseback. Especially not strangers like this man: arrogant. Assuming. Autocratic.

Besides, she had stayed awake most of the last night.

It would not hurt her to stay awake a little longer. She looked up at him as they rode, at the strong line of his jaw under the mask, at the purposeful look in his dark eyes. Then, because she realised she was staring, she looked upwards to where it seemed as if all the stars in the universe had come out to play in a velvet sky.

She picked out the brightest stars, familiar stars that she had seen from her suite's balcony at home in the palace.

'Is it far to Jemeya?'

'Too far to travel tonight.'

'But my father, he will know I am safe?'

'He will know.'

'Good.' She yawned again, suddenly bone weary. The night air was cold around her face and she snuggled her face deeper under the cover of the cloak, imagining herself back in her own bed at the palace. That was warm too, a refuge when the winds spun around and carried the chill from the mainland's cold desert nights.

The horse galloped on, rocking her with every stride, but she knew there was no risk of falling, not with this man's arms surrounding her, the cloak wound tightly around them both, anchoring her to his body. She breathed in the warm air against his body, deliciously warm. His scent was so different from her father's familiar blend of aftershave and pipe tobacco, which shouldn't smell good but still did; this man smelled different and yet not unpleasantly so. This man seemed to carry the essence of the desert, warm and evocative, combining sunshine and sand, leather and horseflesh, and some indefinable extra ingredient, some musky quality all his own.

She breathed deeply, savouring it, tucking it away in her memory. Soon enough she would be back in her own bed, with familiar scents and sounds, but for now it was no hardship to stay low under the cloak, to drink in the warmth and his scent and let it seep bone deep.

After all, she was safe now. Why shouldn't she relax just a little? Surely it wouldn't hurt to nap just for a moment or two?

She let her eyelids drift closed as she yawned again, and this time she left them closed as she nestled against the hard, warm torso of her rescuer, breathing deeply of his scent, relishing the motion as the horse rocked them together. It wasn't so bad—a nap would refresh her, and soon she would be home with her father again. Nobody would know she had fallen asleep in the arms of a stranger.

And nobody would ever know how much she enjoyed it.

Zoltan Al Farouk bin Shamal knew the precise moment the princess had fallen asleep. She had been fighting it for some time, battling to remain as rigid and stiff in his arms as a plank of wood.

He almost laughed at the thought. She was no plank of wood. He had suspected as much from the first moment he had pulled her into his arms and spread his fingers wide over her belly. A chance manoeuvre and a lucky one, as it happened, designed to drag her close and shut her up before she could raise the alarm, but with the added bonus of discovering first-hand that this princess came with benefits: a softly rounded belly between the jut of hipbones, the delicious curve of waist to hip and the all-important compunction to want to explore further, just to name a few. It had been no hardship to hold her close and feel her flesh tremble with awareness under his hand, even while she attempted to act as if she was unaffected.

Unaffected, at least, until she had given into her baser instincts and jammed her teeth down on his finger.

This time he allowed himself to laugh, a low rumble that he let the passing air carry away. No, there was nothing wooden about her at all.

Especially now.

The rhythm of the horse had seduced her into relaxing, and bit by bit he had felt her resistance waver, her bones soften, until sleep had claimed her and she had unconsciously allowed her body to melt against his.

She felt surprisingly good there, tucked warm and close against his body, relaxed and loose-limbed, all feminine curves and every one of them an invitation to sin.

Exactly like her scandal-ridden sister, from what he had heard. Was this one as free and easy with her favours? It would not surprise him if she were—she had the sultry good looks of the royal women of Jemeya, the eyes that were enough to make a man hard, the lush mouth that promised the response would not be wasted. At her age, she must have had lovers. But at least, unlike her sister, this one had had the sense not to breed.

It would be no hardship making love with this woman. His groin tightened at the prospect. In less than forty-eight hours she would be his. He could wait that long. Maybe duty and this unwanted marriage would have some benefits after all.

Maybe.

As he looked down in the bundle of his arms, one thing he was sure of—spoilt princess or not, she was far too good for the likes of Mustafa.

Around him his friends fanned out, sand flying from the horses' hooves as they sped across the dunes. Better than good friends, they were the brothers he had never had, the brothers he had instead chosen. They would stay for the wedding and the coronation, they had promised, and then they would each go their separate ways again—Kadar back to Istanbul, Bahir to the roulette tables of Monte Carlo and Rashid to wherever in the world he could make the most money in the shortest time.

He would miss them when they were gone, and this time he would not be free to join them whenever the opportunity arose. For he was no longer the head of a global executive-jet fleet with the ability to take off to wherever he wanted if he had the time. Now everything he had built up might have been for nothing. Now he was stuck here in Al-Jirad to do his duty.

The woman in his arms stirred, muttering something as she shifted, angling herself further into him, one hand sliding down his stomach and perilously close to his groin.

He growled into the night air as he felt himself harden, growled when her hand slipped even lower. If she could do this to him when she was asleep, how much more would she be capable of when she was awake?

He could not wait to find out.

CHAPTER TWO

AISHA woke and sat up in bed, confused and still half-dreaming of mysterious desert men with broad shoulders and glinting eyes, of solid, muscled chests and strong arms with which to cradle her.

No. Not men. Just one man who had taken possession of her dreams as if he had a God-given right to.

Ridiculous. Thank God it was the morning after and she would never have to see him again.

She felt a sudden, bewildering pang of regret that she hadn't had the chance to thank him.

Baffling, really. The man had been arrogant beyond belief, he'd laughed at her every chance he'd had, and her father would have no doubt paid him handsomely for rescuing her—and she was actually sorry she hadn't had the chance to thank him?

What mattered now was that she was safe! Relief that they had got away turned to exhilaration running through her veins. She had been rescued from her kidnappers and the sick promise of a marriage to that pig, Mustafa. She let herself collapse back into the pillows with a sigh.

She was free.

She looked around the dimly lit room, searching for clues. Where was she? A palace or a plush hotel, given the dimensions of the room and the opulence of the furnishings. A palace with a bed almost as comfortable as her own at home, a bed she couldn't wait to reacquaint herself with tonight.

She was still wearing her robe, she realised as she slipped from the bed. Whoever had brought her here hadn't bothered to change her, merely put her to bed in the robe she had been wearing when she was rescued.

The man who had cradled her in his arms on his horse?

She stopped, halfway to the window, turned and looked back at the big, wide bed. Had he been here, in this room, leaning over to lay her softly on the bed, cautious not to wake her? Had he gently pulled the soft quilt up to cover her and keep her warm?

She shivered, remembering the warmth of his breath against her cheek when he had held her in the tent, remembering the solid thump of the heartbeat in his chest.

And then she remembered the way he had laughed at her, and she wondered why she was wasting so much time thinking about him when there were far more important things to consider.

Like going home.

She padded to the window, curious for a glimpse outside if only to give her a clue as to where she was. Maybe her father was already here, anxiously waiting for her to wake up so he could greet her.

She curled her toes into a luxurious silk rug as she pushed aside a curtain. She squinted into the bright sunlit day—later than morning, she estimated from the height and power of the sun. How long had she slept?

Blinking, she shielded her eyes with her hand and peered out again, letting her eyes adjust. Below her was a large courtyard garden, filled with orange trees and flowering shrubs, pools of water running between and a fountain in the centre, its splashing water sparkling like diamonds. Around the square ran a cloistered walkway beyond which the palace spread, grand and magnificent, topped with towers and gold domes that shone brightly in the sun. The scene was utterly beautiful.

Except for the black flags that flapped from every flagpole. She shivered in spite of the heat of the day, a sense of foreboding turning her blood cold.

Why were they all black? What had happened?

There was a knock on the door and she turned as a young woman bearing a tray entered, her eye drawn to the window. 'Oh, you're awake, Princess.' She bowed, put the tray down on a table and poured a cup of hot, aromatic liquid. 'You've slept almost the whole day. I've brought tea, some yoghurt and fruit in case you were hungry.'

'Where am I? And why are there black flags flying on the flagpoles?'

The girl looked as if she didn't know how to answer as she held out the cup of steaming beverage. Aisha caught the sweet scent of honey, spices, nutmeg and cinnamon on the steam. 'I will let them know you are awake.'

'Them?' She took a hopeful step closer as she took the cup. 'Is my father here?'

The girl's eyes slid away to a door. 'You have slept a very long time. You will find your clothes in the dressing room. Would you like me to select something for you while you bathe?'

She shook her head and put the cup aside. 'No. I want you to answer my question.'

The girl blinked. 'You are in Al-Jirad, of course.'

Al-Jirad? Then not far from Jemeya. No more than

thirty minutes by helicopter from the coast, an hour from the inland. 'And my father? Is he here, or is he waiting for me at home?'

'Someone will come for you shortly.' The girl bowed, looking uncomfortable and already withdrawing, heading for the door.

'Wait!'

She paused, looking warily over her shoulder. 'Yes?'

'I don't even know your name.'

She nodded meekly and uncertainly, her hands clasped in front of her. 'It is Rani, Princess.'

Aisha smiled, trying to put the girl at ease. She had so many questions and the girl must know something. 'Thank you for the tea, Rani. And, if I might just ask…?'

'Yes?'

'The man who brought me here… I mean the *men* who brought me here. Are they still somewhere in the palace, do you know?'

The girl looked longingly in the direction of the door.

'I wanted to thank them for rescuing me.'

The girl's eyes were large and wide, her small hands knotted tightly together in front of her. 'Someone will come for you, Princess. That is all I can say.' And with a bow she practically fled, her slippered feet almost soundless on the floor, the door snicking quietly closed behind her.

Aisha sighed in frustration as she sipped more of the sweet tea, relieved to know where she was, but still left wondering and worrying about the black flags. Maybe the King's aged mother had finally succumbed to the illness that had plagued her these past few years. The last she had heard, the old queen had not been responding to treatment. The Al-Jiradans would justifiably be sad at her passing, she mused. Queen Petra had been universally loved and adored.

But, beyond that, the knowledge she was in Al-Jirad was welcome. Relations between Al-Jirad and Jemeya—one little more than a patch of bare desert at the end of a sandy peninsular, the other a dot of an island a short distance off-shore—were close and went back centuries. Strategically positioned either side of the only navigable waterway into the desert interior, a deep trench that gave access to shipping, the two had forged a strong bond over the years, their geography assigning them the role of gatekeepers to the inland access route.

And Al-Jirad's King Hamra was one of her father's closest friends and allies. This must be one of the several palaces he had dotted across the kingdom.

She bathed quickly, anxious to find out more, and all the time wondering why she'd bothered to ask the girl about her rescuers. Would she really want to see him again, even if he was still in the palace, knowing how he had affected her? Did she really want to thank him?

Because how could she face him and not remember how intimately he had held her? How could she stop herself from blushing when she remembered how good—and, at the same time, how disturbing—it had felt?

No. She dried herself and slipped into a gown hanging in the bathroom. It was better they remained strangers. It was just as well he had never taken off his mask and she had never seen his face. It was far better she had no idea who he was.

She paused by the tray and nibbled on a fat, juicy date while she poured herself more tea, savouring the sweet, spicy brew, feeling more human after her shower and confident that soon she would be on her way home.

Then she pulled open the dressing-room doors to find something to wear.

And felt the sizzle all the way down her spine to her toes.

The relief she'd been feeling at being rescued, the relief at finally being safe, started unravelling from the warm ball of contentment in her gut and twisted, tangled and knotted into something far more ominous.

Because the wardrobe she'd been expecting to hold one or two items was full.

Of her own clothes.

Her own gowns and robes met her gaze, her own shoes, slippers and purses. She gazed around the walls of the room, at the shelves and the mirrored recesses where her jewellery box sat in pride of place. Even Honey—the tiny teddy bear she'd had as a child, its ears shiny and bare after years of stroking them with her thumb as she fell asleep—sat jauntily winking at her with his one remaining eye from on top of a chest of drawers. She picked up the worn, well-loved toy and held it to her breast, wishing for the comfort it had always lent as a child before dropping to a sofa, confusion scrambling her brain.

'What does it mean, Honey?' she whispered quietly to her toy, just as she had done as a child when she could not understand what was going on in the grown-up world around her. Just as she had done when her father had told her that her mother was never coming home from the hospital where she had gone to have a baby. 'Why?'

Part of her wanted to run like that child had run, find the girl called Rani and ask her, demand to know this instant, what was happening, what it was she wasn't telling her. But she was an adult now, and a princess, and could hardly go running around a palace in a dressing gown.

No, that way was not her way, no matter how confused she felt, no matter how much she needed answers to her questions. Besides, there had to be a logical explanation for why all her things had been shipped to a palace somewhere in Al-Jirad. There had to be.

So she would not make a spectacle of herself. She would choose something from her own clothes, get dressed, and only then, when she looked like the princess she was, would she go looking for answers.

And she intended to find them!

A man calling himself Hamzah came for her one interminable hour later. The Sheikh's vizier, he had told her, bowing deeply, and when she had started to question him he had promised that the Sheikh would answer all her questions. So she duly followed the wiry old man along the shaded cloister she had seen from her window, her impatience building by the minute.

The sun was lower now, turning the golden stone of the palace to a burnished red, though it was still almost too hot for the white linen trouser suit she had selected from her wardrobe.

She didn't care. She had chosen smart travelling clothes over one of her cooler silk abayas for a reason: she wanted it to be clear that she intended travelling home to Jemeya the first chance she got, today if it was at all possible. They could pack up and send her clothes after her.

The merest hint of a breeze, cooled by the fountains and the garden, tickled the patch of bare skin behind her neck, making her thankful she'd knotted her hair behind her head. Cool serenity she had been aiming for in her look, which was what she most needed. Along with confidence. Which she had for the most part, she felt, until she thought about the mystery of the clothes so neatly filling the dressing room and the absence of any kind of answers to her questions.

The strangeness of it all once again sent skitters down her spine. No matter how much she had tried to find a logical reason, to try to explain what possible reason they had sent her entire wardrobe here, it made no sense at all.

She shivered despite the warmth of the day, the relief she'd felt at escaping Mustafa's desert camp rapidly dissipating in the wake of all of her unanswered questions.

And in the shadow of a growing suspicion.

Something was wrong.

The vizier led her deeper into the palace, through a maze of corridors; between walls lined with beautiful mosaics set with gemstones, the colours leaping out at her; past rich wall-hangings and tapestries of animals frolicking on the banks of rivers. And water, water was always a theme—in the murals, mosaics and in the tiny fountains, trickling from stone jars in every corner over rocks, making music with water.

It was beautiful.

No doubt designed to be quite restful.

If you weren't already seething with impatience, turning every watery tinkle, every babbling and burbling rivulet, into the sound of someone scraping their nails down a blackboard.

By the time they came to a set of carved doors that rose imposing and ominous before them, she was ready to scrape her nails down anything.

Strange; she wasn't normally a violent person or prone to biting or scratching.

'Can you run as hard as you bite?'

She remembered the laughter in his words and she wished she'd bitten down harder. Then Hamzah beckoned her to follow, and she promised to put that man out of her mind once and for all. He was gone, probably busy blowing his reward at the nearest casino or fleshpot.

Mercenaries would be like that, she figured. In it for the money. The thrill of the hunt. The quick buck.

They entered a library, the floor and columns of the massive room decked in marble, smooth and cool, the occasional chairs and tables gilt and inlaid with precious stones, the walls lined with books and manuscripts. And there, in one far corner of the room, sat a man behind a computer, his hair shining blue-black under the lights.

He looked up as they approached, his eyes narrowing as he sat back in his chair. A secretary, she assumed with a sigh, wondering how long it would be and how many more layers of bureaucracy she would encounter until finally she found this mysterious sheikh and maybe even someone who could answer her questions.

'Princess Aisha.'

She stepped forward, her patience having reached its limit. 'Can you answer my questions? Or can you at least point me in the direction of someone who can? Because, as much as I am grateful for your hospitality, I need to know why I am not already on my way home to Jemeya but instead find the wardrobe in my room stuffed full of my clothes.'

The older man reared back as if he'd been physically struck. 'Excellency, I am sorry.'

Her eyes snapped around to the vizier. *Excellency?*

'Thank you, Hamzah. I'll handle this now.' And something in his voice made her turn back to the man in the chair, even while the older man withdrew. Almost in slow motion, it seemed, he pushed back his chair and rose to his full height.

Tall, she registered. Broad-shouldered.

And there was something about that voice…

Her mouth went dry.

It could not be him! She must be going mad if she imagined this man to be her rescuer. That man was a mercenary, sent by her father to rescue her. And this man was some kind of…*royalty*?

'Why did he call you Excellency? Surely that term is reserved for King Hamra, the ruler of Al-Jirad?'

She swallowed as he rounded the desk, long-limbed and lean, before propping himself against it, crossing his arms over his broad chest as he coolly surveyed her with dark, unreadable eyes. His hard face was constructed of too many harsh angles and too many dark places to be considered conventionally handsome. And, with the dark blue-black shadow of his beard, he looked—dangerous.

'So, who are you?' she asked, raising her chin in defiance, willing her voice not to crack. 'Why is it so impossible to get answers to my questions?'

'You are impatient, Princess. I was not warned of that particular trait. But then, I suppose you have been through an ordeal and we can excuse it this once. Did you sleep well?'

She was impatient but he could excuse it *just this once*. Who the hell did he think he was? What was it about Al-Jirad and the men here that brought out the worst in them? 'And I am expected to answer your questions while you choose not to answer mine?'

He smiled then, and for a moment he almost looked human. Almost. Before his face reverted to dark, shadowed planes and grim eyes. 'Touché.' He gave just the merest inclination of his head. 'I am Sheikh Zoltan Al Farouk bin Shamal, but of course you may call me Zoltan.'

'And I am Princess Aisha of the royal Peshwah family of Jemeya, and you may address me as Princess Aisha.'

This time he laughed, a rich, deep sound that sounded far too good to come from someone like him, a man she wanted to dislike everything about.

'Where is my father?' she demanded, cutting his laughter short. 'Why is he not here to greet me? I was promised he would know I was safe, but instead I find myself still here in Al-Jirad, instead of already being on my way home to Jemeya.'

He spread his arms out wide. 'You have an issue with your suite? Have we not made you comfortable here? Is there anything you lack?'

'I was assured my father would know I was safe.'

'And he knows, Princess Aisha. As he has known since you were plucked from that desert encampment last night. I spoke to him again once you were safe within this palace's walls. He is overjoyed beyond measure. He wanted me to tell you that.'

She blew out a breath she hadn't realised she'd been holding. At least something made sense. They were the exact words she would expect her father to use. 'So he's still in Jemeya, then, waiting for me to return home.' It still didn't explain why he would send her entire wardrobe—surely her lady in waiting could have selected a few likely outfits for her to choose from? But maybe he panicked.

'No. He is not in Jemeya, but right here in Al Jirad,

at the Blue Palace, attending to some business. He will be here tomorrow.'

She blinked. The Blue Palace was the ceremonial palace of Al-Jirad, and the seat of the kingdom. Her father must have business with the King. But then she remembered the black flags flying atop the palace roof. Of course he would be here in Al-Jirad at such a time. 'Did something happen to Queen Petra? There are black flags flying.'

His brow furrowed, his eyes narrowing, drawing her eye to the strong black lashes framing his dark eyes. 'Yes, as it happens. It did.'

'Oh,' she said, 'that's so sad. So I'm not leaving just yet.'

He smiled again. 'No, Princess, you are not.'

'Then I will just have to wait for him here.'

He smiled and crossed his ankles, drawing her eye to the long, lean line of his legs encased in what looked like the finest fabric, superbly tailored. Superbly fitted everywhere. 'I get the impression you are not used to waiting, Princess.'

She realised she was staring, and where, and snapped her eyes back to his face. She caught a glimmer of laughter in the crease of his eyes and the curve of his lips. Laughter, and something entirely more menacing, and she got the impression he thought he was toying with her, like a cat with a mouse, prodding it one way and then the other, wanting it to run so he could pounce...

Well, she was no mouse and she would not run. And, sheikh or no sheikh, she didn't like his tone, nor his words that told her he was busy adding to her list of character faults. As if it mattered to her what he thought of her. She stiffened her spine.

'Maybe it's because I seem to have done nothing else lately. I spent many hours out in the desert, waiting for escape. But I can wait one more night.'

He nodded, his smile growing wider. 'Excellent. I am sure you will find your time here most entertaining.'

She sensed she was being dismissed, and she realised that she was doing most of the 'entertaining', for he seemed more than amused. But she also realised that, no matter how much the man irritated her, she could not go without at least thanking him for offering her a safe haven. 'Then thank you, Sheikh Zoltan, for your hospitality. I apologise if I seemed impatient earlier but naturally I became frustrated when nobody seemed willing or able to answer my questions.'

'Perfectly understandable, Princess. You have been through a testing time.'

She nodded and gave a matter-of-fact smile, relieved she hadn't plunged their two countries into some kind of diplomatic crisis. After all, she was being offered protection here in a neighbouring country. Sanctuary. She should not abuse that courtesy. 'Then I will not waste any more of your time, Sheikh Zoltan. I will wait in my suite until my father arrives.'

He took her hand and she felt a sizzle of recognition, of having held a hand like this one before, a hand that belonged to a man who ran with long, powerful strides...

Impossible!

'Tell me one thing,' she said, disturbed enough to remember another niggling question that had not been answered. 'Why did my father send all of my belongings here when I will be in Al-Jirad such a short time? Surely he must have realised I could have made do with a suitcase-full at the most? Why do you think he did that?'

He shrugged, her hand still wrapped securely in his. 'Maybe he thought you would need them afterwards.'

'Afterwards? After what?'

'After we are married, of course.'

CHAPTER THREE

SHE wrenched her hand away. 'You must be mad!' The entire world must be going crazy! First Mustafa and now this man claiming she must marry him! 'I'm not marrying anyone,' she said, wanting to laugh so insanely at the very idea that maybe *she* was the one who was mad. 'Not Mustafa. And certainly not you.'

'I am sorry to break the news this way, Princess. I had intended to invite you to dine with me tonight, and convince you of the merits of the scheme while I seduced you with the best food, wine and entertainment that Al-Jirad can offer.'

'It does not matter how you planned the delivery. Your message would still be insane and my answer would still be the same. I am not marrying you! And now I intend to return to my suite and await the arrival of my father. I'm sorry that someone went to the trouble of unpacking all my belongings when they will only have to repack it all for the journey home tomorrow. Good night.'

She wheeled around, already taking a step towards the door that looked a million miles away right now, when her wrist was seized in an iron clasp.

'Not so fast, Princess.'

She looked down to where his hand curled around

her slender wrist, his skin a dark golden-olive, making her own honey-coloured skin pale to almost white. Or was that just because all her blood had drained away and turned her ghostlike?

She lifted her gaze to his dark, glinting eyes. 'Nobody touches a princess of Jemeya without consent.'

'Surely the betrothed…'

She pulled her wrist from his grip. 'I have no betrothed!'

'That's not what your father thinks.'

'Then you *are* indeed crazy. My father would never give his permission for a marriage I did not want.'

'Maybe your father has no choice.'

'And maybe you're dreaming. For when he arrives tomorrow he will surely set you straight. He did not send his men to rescue me from the hands of one mad despot to simply hand me over to another.'

'You are so sure they were your father's men?'

His words blindsided her. What kind of question was that? Of course her father had sent her rescuers. 'They came for me,' she asserted, hating this man right now for making her question her own father's actions, for making her doubt that he would do anything and everything in his power to get her back. 'As I knew they would from the first moment I was kidnapped. I knew my father would send someone to rescue me and I was right. And they told me that my father would be told I was safe. So who else would have sent them?'

'And if I told you that it was my men who rescued you from that desert camp and from a future bearing Mustafa's fat and plentiful sons?'

She threw her hands up in the air. 'I've heard enough of this. I'm leaving.' She turned away and started walking. She was going to walk out of here and through that door, and this time, when she did, she would forget all about being a princess and looking like a princess and acting like a princess—she would run as fast and hard as she could back to her suite and lock the door behind her. And she did not care who might see her, or what they might think of her, and she would not come out until her father had arrived and ensured her safe passage back to Jemeya.

This time there was no iron manacle around her wrist, no move to stop her. And for a moment she even thought she might make it. Until she heard him utter the fateful words behind her.

'And if I said I came for you with your father's blessing?'

Her feet shuddered to a halt on the marble-tiled floor, fear clamping down so hard on her muscles that it was impossible to move. She was suddenly aware of the pounding of her blood, her heart racing like that tiny mouse's must have, knowing the cat was behind it, ready to pounce if she moved so much as a tiny whisker.

I came for you?

Did he mean what he had said? Had he been there after all last night? Had he been one of the men in the rescuer's party? Or had he been the one to slice his way into her tent, to plaster her to his body too tightly and set off a low, burning heat deep in her belly, to cradle her in his arms as his stallion galloped across the dunes?

For that man had been tall and broad, supremely fit and sure of himself and unbearably arrogant with it. Yet her rescuer had been a mercenary, dressed all in black, his face completely covered but for his dark, glinting eyes.

No, it couldn't be him. She would not allow it.

She spun around. 'You are bluffing! You admit

speaking to my father this morning. He told you about the rescue and now you try to make me feel so indebted to you, so happy to have escaped the clutches of Mustafa, that I will agree to this—' she searched frantically for a word that might convey just how crazy this marriage idea was '—insanity!'

Not a chance.

'But by all means,' she continued, 'do share this little fantasy of yours with my father when he arrives tomorrow. I'm sure he'll be most entertained.'

Zoltan pushed himself from the edge of the desk, then strode towards her with long, purposeful strides that ate up the distance between them until he stood before her, tall and impossibly autocratic, his eyes fixed with a steely determination, his jaw set like concrete. 'If you want to talk fantasy, Princess, let me share one with you right now. Would you be similarly entertained if I told you that I cannot wait to see what that mouth of yours can do when you are in the throes of passion rather than in the grip of fear?'

Shock thunderbolted down her spine, ricocheted out to her extremities and made her clenching and unclenching hand itch to slap one darkly shadowed cheek. 'How dare you speak to me like that?'

'How dare I?' He reached out a hand, put the pad of his thumb to her lip. 'But you're the one who put the idea into my head, Princess—you and those sharp, white teeth of yours.'

She gasped, took a step back. 'You!'

And then he smiled and, seemingly casually, crossed his arms over his chest. She saw it then, on the index finger of his right hand: the imprint of her teeth etched deep and angry-looking on his skin.

He watched her eyes widen. He saw the realisation dawn and bloom. He smelt her fear.

And it felt strangely good.

'Yes, Princess. Me. Wearing your brand, it would appear—some quaint Jemeyan custom, I assume, to mark one's intended?'

She looked back up at him, her features tight and determined. 'It doesn't matter who you are or whether you were there last night. It doesn't matter if you were in the party that rescued me from that desert camp. I owe you nothing but my thanks, and you have that. But there is still no way I will marry you. And there is no way on this earth that you can make me.'

'You can fight this all you like, Princess, but there is no other way.'

'And if I still say no?'

He smiled. 'In that case, if you feel that strongly, maybe there is one other way after all.'

'Yes?'

'I can take you back to that desert encampment, leave you there and let Mustafa have his way with you. Your choice, Princess.'

She looked as if she was going to explode, face red with heat, her hands clenched at her side and her eyes so alight they were all but throwing flames. 'When my father finishes his business with the King and comes for me tomorrow, he will tell you the same as I do. There will be no marriage!'

All of a sudden he was tired of the game, of baiting her for her reactions, of toying with this spoilt princess, even though she had provided the only entertainment value in a world suddenly turned upon its head. The need to rescue her had brought him and his three friends together again for the first time in five years, and plucking her from beneath the nose of his hated half-brother had presented a moment of such sublime satisfaction that he would revel in the victory for years to come.

Except now he was faced with a precocious, precious princess who thought she had actually some say in what was happening. Why had he ever let her think that? Why had he tolerated her demands, deflected her questions and allowed her that privilege when she had never had it?

He knew damned well why—because he was still so angry about being put in this invidious position himself. Because he couldn't see why he should be the only one to suffer and sacrifice, the only one mightily frustrated at the choiceless situation he found himself thrust into. So why the hell shouldn't he extract some measure of glee from seeing her tossed right out of her precious, princessly comfort-zone?

And what right had she to feel so mightily aggrieved when marriage was the only thing required of her? Whereas his marriage to her was only one tiresome necessity in a long list of requirements his vizier had put before him in order to enable him to take the throne of Al-Jirad. And who had the time for any of this? The ability to speak fluent Jiradi as well as Arabic; the need to be able to quote from the sacred book of Jiradi which he must learn by heart before the coronation; having to honour the alliance between commitment to replenish the blood stock of Al-Jirad with a princess of noble birth from their sister state of Jemeya.

No. Suddenly he was tired of it all.

He sighed as she looked up at him, eyes defiant and openly hostile. He was sick of this whole damn situation before it had even properly begun.

'King Hamra is dead.'

She blinked. Once. Again. And then it seemed her entire face turned into a question mark, eyes wide, mouth open in shock. Then she shook her head. 'No.' Her hands flew to her mouth. 'You said it was Queen Petra. No!'

He watched those hands. He remembered them. Slim, he recalled. Long-fingered. Hands that had come perilously close to grazing the fabric covering his swelling organ last night. Hands that would soon have that privilege and that right, a right he hoped they would soon exercise.

Then he noticed her eyes and found them already filling with tears, threatening to spill over. He simultaneously wondered at her ability to distract him and cursed it when he knew the news he had to deliver was only going to make her feel worse. 'But how?' she cried. 'When?'

'The morning before you were kidnapped. King Hamra was on his way to Egypt for a holiday— he and the Queen in one helicopter with his close advisers, his mother and sons, their wives and families in the other. For some reason the two helicopters ventured too close to each other. Nobody knows why. But it seems that their blades touched and both helicopters plummeted to the ground.'

He gave her a moment to let the news sink in before he added, 'There were no survivors.'

Her face was almost devoid of colour, her dark eyes and lashes suddenly starkly standing out on a skin so deathly pale that he worried she might actually collapse.

He took hold of her shoulders before she might fall and steered her to the nearest chair where she sagged, limp and boneless.

'But surely not all of them? Not Akram and Renata?

Not Kaleem and Akra? And, please, no, surely not the children? They were so young, just babies…'

He could offer her nothing, so he said nothing, just gave the slightest shake of his head.

'Nobody told me!' she cried when she realised the truth and the extent of the disaster. 'I knew nothing. All the time I was in that desert camp they told me nothing. Oh yes, they laughed and smirked and made crude jokes about what Mustafa intended to do with me, but nobody told me that the King and his family had been killed. Nobody told me…'

She looked up at him, the shock, hurt and misery right there in her eyes to see, and for a moment he almost felt sorry for her and sorry for the upset all this damned mess would cause her. But, hell, why should he feel sorry for her, when his life had been similarly turned upside down, his future curtailed by the rules laid down by those of centuries past? The fact was that they were both the victims in this situation.

'Is this why all this is happening? Because it is somehow connected to that tragedy?'

Why did she have to look so damned vulnerable? He wanted to be angry with her, the spoilt princess who was having to do what her nation needed instead of what she wanted for a change. The last thing on earth he wanted was to feel empathy for her. To feel sorry. Especially when he was being subjected to the same external forces. He sucked in air. 'Al-Jirad needs a king.'

She looked up at him through glassy eyes, her long black lashes heavy with tears. 'That man—the vizier—he called you Excellency. Are you to be that king?'

'I am one possibility. King Hamra was my uncle. My father had two sons to two different wives. One was Mustafa. The other was me.' He paused. 'And, of course, whichever one of us it is to be is decided by the pact.'

She nodded, her eyes hardening with the realisation of what this came down to, the grief still there, but framed in anger now. 'So that's what this is all about, then, this game of Hunt the Princess. Whoever marries the princess first wins the crown of Al-Jirad.'

'It is what the pact requires. Where the crown of Al-Jirad is compromised, the alliance will be renewed by the marriage between the royal families of our two countries. Because of your older sister's situation…'

'You mean, because she has two children to two different fathers and she never actually bothered marrying either of them, she's no longer eligible for the position? But surely she has a proven track-record. If it's heirs you need—and when has any monarchy not been all about heirs?—Marina has proven child-bearing capabilities, where sadly I do not.'

'Your sister is, to put it mildly, over-qualified for the position. The fact you have not yet bred is still in your favour.'

Have not yet bred. She itched to hit something. Anything. Maybe him. Except princesses were not supposed to do such things, were not expected to give in to such base instincts. But still, the claim that this agreement was somehow in her favour rubbed, and rubbed raw.

'How can it be in my favour when it forces me into this situation?'

'It is duty, Princess. It is not personal.'

Not personal? Maybe that was why she hated it so much. Because it wasn't personal. And she had dreamed—oh, how she had dreamed—that being so far down the line to the crown, and a woman into the deal, would ensure she would never be subjected to the strictures of the first or even the second-born sons. She had watched her brothers with their tutors, seen how little rope they had been given. And she had watched her sister, who had been given too much too quickly while all the attention was on her brothers and their futures. She had been foolish enough to think she could somehow escape the madness of it all unscathed and lead a near-normal life. She had stupidly hoped she might even marry for love.

Zoltan watched her as she sat there, trying to absorb the enormity of the situation that confronted her. But it was hardly the end of the world, as she made it out to be. He would be the one on the throne, a position he'd never been prepared for, whereas she would go from princess to queen, a job she'd been primed for her entire life. What was so difficult about that?

They could still have a decent enough marriage if they both wanted. She was beautiful, this princess, long-limbed and lithe, with skin like satin. It would be no hardship at all to bed her to procure the heirs Al-Jirad required. And she had a fire burning beneath that cool, princessly exterior, a fire he was curious to discover more about, a fire he was keen to stoke for himself.

Why shouldn't it work, at least in the bedroom? And, if it didn't, then there were ways and means around that. An heir and a spare and they both would have done their duty; they could both look at different options. So just because they had to marry didn't make it a death sentence.

Then she shook her head, rising to her feet and brushing at the creases in her trousers, and he got the impression she would just as simply brush away the obligations laid upon her by the pact between their two countries.

And just as fruitlessly.

'So marrying you is to be my fate, then, decided by some crusty piece of paper that is hundreds of years old?'

'The pact sets out what must happen in the event of a situation such as this.'

'And of course we all must do what the pact says we must do.'

'It is the foundation stone of both our countries' constitutions—you know that. Are you so averse to doing your duty as a princess of one of those two countries?'

'Yes! Of course I am, if it means my fate is to marry either you or Mustafa! Of course I object.'

'Then maybe it is just as well you do not have a choice in the matter.'

'I refuse to believe that. What if I simply refuse to marry either of you? What if I have other plans for my life that don't include being married to some despot who thinks he can lay claim to a woman merely because of an accident of her birth?'

'That *accident of birth*, as you put it, gives you much wealth and many privileges, Princess. But it also comes with responsibilities. Your sister chose to shrug them off. Being the only other member of the royal Jemeyan family who can satisfy the terms of the pact, you do not have that option.'

'You can't make me marry you. I can still say no and I *do* say no.'

'Like I said, that is not an option available to you.'

She shrieked, a brittle sound of frustration and exasperation, her hands curled into tight, tense fists at her side. He yawned and looked at his watch. Any moment now he expected she would stamp her feet, maybe even throw herself to the floor and pound the tiles with her curled-up fists like a spoilt child. Not that it would do her any good.

'Look,' she started, the spark in her eye telling him she'd hit on some new plan of attack. Her hands unwound and she took a deep breath. She even smiled, if you could call it that. At least, it was the closest thing to a smile he'd seen her give to date. 'This is all so unnecessary. The pact is centuries old and we've all moved on a long way since then. There must be some misunderstanding.'

'You think?'

'I know.' She held out her hands as if she was preaching. Maybe she thought she was, because she was suddenly fired up with her building argument, her eyes bright, her features alive. He was struck again with how beautiful she was, how fine her features, how lush her mouth. His groin stirred. No, it would be no hardship bedding her. No hardship at all.

'My father loves me. He would never make me marry a man I didn't love, not for anything.'

'Not for anything?' He arched an eyebrow. 'Not even for the continuing alliance between our two countries?'

'So, maybe…' she said, with sparks in her eyes, really getting into it, 'maybe it's time we drew up a new agreement. Times have changed. The world has moved on. We could lead our respective countries into a new future, with a new and better alliance, something more applicable to the modern era that covers communication and the Internet and today's world instead of one that doesn't exist any more.'

He crossed his arms, nodded, fought to keep the smile from his own face as he pretended to give it serious thought. 'A new agreement? I can see how that would appeal.'

She failed or chose to ignore the sarcasm dripping from his words. 'Besides, of course, there is my work in Jemeya. My father would not expect me to walk away from my duties there.'

'Ah, yes, your *work*. Of course, someone like you would consider sitting down with a bunch of homeless kids and reading them fairy stories to be work. Very valuable work, no doubt. Makes for a few good photo opportunities, I dare say.'

Her eyes glinted, the smile wiped clean from her face. 'I teach them our language! I teach them how to read and write!'

'And nobody else in Jemeya can do that? Face facts, Princess.' He kicked himself away from the column. 'You are needed by Jemeya as much as a finger needs a wart.'

'How dare you?'

'I dare because someone needs to tell you. Jemeya does not need you, and the sooner you face facts the better. You have two older brothers, one of whom will inherit the throne, the other a spare if he cannot. So what good are you to Jemeya? Don't you see? You are surplus to requirements. You're a redundant princess. So you might as well be of some use to your country by marrying me.'

Her eyes were still glinting but now it was with ice-cold hatred.

'I have told you—I will not marry you and my father will not make me. Why would anyone in their right mind want to marry you? You led me to believe I had been rescued from one mad man when all along you were planning captivity of the same kind with another.

'Maybe it's time you faced facts yourself—you're arrogant beyond belief, you're a bully and you're so anxious to be Al-Jirad's next king that you would stop at nothing to get on that throne. I won't marry you now and I wouldn't marry you if you were the last man left on earth!'

Blood pounded in his temples, pounding out a drumbeat of fury, sounding out a call to war. What must he have done wrong in some former life that he would be lumbered with this selfish little princess for a wife? What gods had he somewhere and at some time insulted that they would visit upon him this poisoned shrew? For if he had a choice right now, if he didn't know Mustafa would otherwise get the crown, he would take her back and dump her back in that desert camp and be finished with her.

'Do you actually believe that I want to be king? Do you actually think that even if I wanted a wife I would want to marry someone who does not know when she is being offered the better end of the deal? Do you really think I want to marry such a spoilt, selfish little shrew?'

'Bastard!' He heard the crack, felt the sting of her hand hard across his cheek, and the blood in his pounding veins turned molten.

He seized her wrist as it flashed by, wrenching her to him. 'You'll pay for that!' She tried to pull her arm free and when he did not let go she pounded his chest with her free hand, twisting her shoulders from side to side.

'Let me go.'

Like hell.

He grabbed her other wrist, and she shrieked and tugged so hard against his restraint until she shook the hair loose behind her head and sent it tumbling down in disarray. 'Let me *go*!'

'Why?' he ground out between clenched teeth. 'So you can slap me again?'

But she twisted one arm right around, her wrist somehow slipped free and she raised it to lash at him again. He caught it this time before she could strike and pulled her in close to his body, trapping her arm under his and bringing her face within inches of his own. She was breathing hard, as if she'd just sprinted a mile, her chest rising and falling fast and furiously against his, her eyes spitting fire at him, her lips parted, gasping for air and showing those neat, sharp teeth, whose bite he could still feel on his hand.

He looked at her mouth and wondered how she would taste   something spicy and sweet with a chili bite. He looked at those wide, lush lips, parted like an invitation, looked at the teeth again and decided it might even be worth the risk.

And then he shifted his gaze and realised she was watching him watching her, her eyes wide, her pupils so dilated they were turning her eyes black.

'I hate you!' she spat, twisting her body against his, friction turning to heat, heat turning to desire.

Desire combusting to need.

'I know,' he said, breathing just as hard and fast. 'I hate you too.' Before his mouth crashed down hard on hers.

And even as she turned rigid beneath him, even though shock stilled her muscles, he felt the warmth of her blossoming heat beneath his kiss, tasted the honey and spice he knew he'd find there, tasted the chili heat—and there, in the midst of the honey, cinnamon and chili, he tasted the promise of a woman beneath the princess.

And he wanted more.

CHAPTER FOUR

SHOCK punched the air from her lungs, sent all thoughts scattering from her mind. But God, she could still feel!

He seemed to be everywhere, the strong wall of his chest pressed hard against her, the steel bands of his arms surrounding her, the rough of his whiskered cheek against her skin and the press of his lips against her own.

Even the very air that intermingled between them, their heated breath, seemed full of his essence, his taste.

And for a moment that recognition blindsided her because it was so powerful. She did recognise his scent and the very feel of him, and she knew it was truly him—the man who had cradled her tightly in his arms, whose chest she had turned into to breathe more of him in while his horse had carried her away from the desert camp and away from that slug, Mustafa, who thought he could just take her at will...

Revulsion blossomed inside her, welling up like a mushroom cloud, giving her frozen limbs strength and purpose and her blank mind the will to act.

She thrust her chin up, twisted her face away, seeking escape from his relentless kiss. 'No,' she cried. *'No!'*

But he did not stop. He gave her no space, no release. He showed no mercy. Instead she felt herself lifted from her feet and swung around until she felt the hard marble of a column at her back. She felt herself sandwiched between it and him, pinning her to his long, lean body while his seeking mouth found hers again and she was full of him and the taste of him. Coaxing. Demanding. Persuading.

So persuasive.

Her body stirred. Her body responded, and she hated herself for it, even as she angled her head to give his mouth and his hot tongue better access to her mouth.

Then his hand slid down her arm, brushed one aching nipple on a straining breast, and suddenly it was Mustafa's greasy fingers she saw in her mind's eye, it was the smack of *his* lips as he walked towards her...

Oh God.

And that image was enough to give her the strength she needed. 'No!' she cried, twisting hard against the steel-hard shackles of his strong limbs. 'Get away from me!' And somehow she managed to unleash one wild hand and lashed out with it to push him away, her nails finding purchase on flesh as she dragged them down.

She heard his curse and suddenly she found herself thrust away, panting and reeling and having to search for the bones in her legs in order to stay upright while he stood there looking like a thundercloud, dark, grim and threatening, rubbing his scored cheek. She waited, gasping for air, shocked by what she had done, appalled that she, a princess of the royal house of Jemeya, had performed such a base act. Yet she was not sorry she had done it. Not one bit.

But she was afraid.

The reality of her position was never starker, never more terrifying. For she was alone in this palace, with no allies, no-one to protect her. He was big, powerful and angry, and she had struck him and drawn blood. The way his chest heaved, the way his pulse pounded angrily at his temples and his eyes looked wild and vengeful, she knew he would not let her get away with that.

Just when she feared he would act, that he might actually raise his hand to strike her, he surprised her by smiling, a long, lazy crocodile smile. 'What quaint customs you Jemeyans have. What does this second brand signify, I wonder? Eternal fidelity? Ever-lasting love? Or a promise of many years of wild, passionate nights in my bed?'

'You flatter yourself! You know exactly why I hit you. How else was I supposed to make you stop acting like a barbarian?'

'Maybe it was not clear you wanted to stop.' And, maybe because he saw the disbelief etched so clearly on her features, he added for good measure, 'Your body told me you did not want to stop.'

'Then you weren't listening!'

He lifted his hand, exposing the three angry red lines marring his cheek, his eyes widening at the blood smeared on his hand. 'You will be sorry for this.'

She almost laughed out loud. His threat meant nothing to her. 'No. I don't think so. What I'm actually sorry about is for assuming I was being rescued last night rather than being kidnapped into some other nightmare. I'm sorry for having to listen to this ridiculous scheme of yours and argue its insanity, and I'm really sorry you do not seem to have any concept of how mad you are. But I am not sorry for hitting you. You asked for that!'

His lip curled. 'I should take you back to Mustafa's camp and leave you there.'

Fear crawled up her spine, even though she knew that

there was no chance of it, even though she knew that he would never do such a thing—not when he wanted the throne for himself. Yet still she remembered the old crone's probing fingers, the humiliating inspection, and she remembered what Mustafa had promised to do to her the moment they were married and he was safe...

'My half-brother deserves a woman like you,' Zoltan continued. 'He deserves someone who can give him grief and make his life hell.'

But the poison of his insults washed off her, only serving to fuel the fire in her veins. She tossed her hair back, refusing to be cowed by his kind. 'If you think you're so different from him you are kidding yourself mightily.'

His face turned as red as a pomegranate, the tendons in his neck standing out in thick, tight cords, his pulse dancing in his throat. 'I am *nothing* like him!'

'Then you don't know him at all. You are both contemptible! Unfit to rule a line, let alone an entire kingdom. Al Jirad is better off without the both of you.'

'Then who will be king?'

'I don't care. Someone else can sort that out. But I tell you this much, just as I'll tell my father when he comes: I am not marrying either of you.'

'You do that, Princess. You tell your father. You tell yourself. You tell whoever you like. Maybe if you say it often enough, you might even believe it.

'But you would be wasting your breath. For in less than twenty-four hours we will be married, whether you like it or not.'

'Over my dead body!'

His eyes glinted dangerously, the three scratches down his cheek standing out bold and angry. 'If that's what it takes.'

If the vizier hadn't chosen that exact moment to arrive, she would have hit him again—harder this time.

Princesses didn't hit, she knew. Princesses were serene, kept their cool and never lashed out—so she had been taught by endless tutors. But she had grown up with older brothers. They might have been princes, but they'd certainly not treated her and her sister like princesses. Oh yes, she was more than capable of dealing with bullies.

'Hamzah,' he said to the bowing vizier. 'What is it?'

The vizier took one look at Zoltan's cheek before glancing over at Aisha with disdain, taking in her unkempt hair, her reddened cheeks, clearly disapproving of what he saw. Then he blinked as if she didn't matter and turned back to Sheikh Zoltan.

'Sheikh King Ashar has called from the Blue Palace. He asks if he can speak to the princess.'

At last! Zoltan looked at her and now it was her turn to smile, because finally this was her moment. The sooner she spoke to her father, the sooner a halt could be put to these crazy wedding plans. Finally she had a chance to talk to someone who would listen to her, someone who cared about her, rather than trying to reason with a man who was like a brick wall and gave not a toss for what she wanted. 'Where can I take the call?'

When the vizier bowed and gestured towards the big desk in the corner, it was all she could do not to run over and snatch up the receiver simply to hear her father's voice again, just to let him know that, while she might be safe from one despot, it was only to be landed in the lap of another. He could not know the full details of what was planned. He must have been deceived. He must have no idea what this man was really planning.

But she wouldn't let herself run across the floor to

the phone. She could do serene when she wanted to, she could do regal. She was just finding it *harder* when this man was around, the urge to act rather than think decidedly more tempting.

'We will leave you in privacy, Princess,' Zoltan said behind her, about to withdraw after Hamzah. On a wicked whim she turned and held up one hand, one-hundred-per-cent confident in what her father would say.

'No. You wait. I'm sure you will be interested in what my father has to say.'

For as much as she hated him, as much as he threw her off-balance, she wanted him here to witness this, she wanted no more misunderstandings between them. Finally she could talk to her father, someone reasonable, someone who made sense and cared about her as a person, not just as some chattel to be exchanged in a business deal. And afterwards she would hand the phone over so her father could tell Zoltan the same thing because he would surely not believe her. She picked up the receiver, still smiling. God, after what she'd been through, she was really going to enjoy this. 'Papa, it's so good to talk to you!'

She listened and laughed as he expressed his delight, thanks and apologies for not being there to meet her. She assured him that she was unharmed, that neither Mustafa nor his men had hurt her, not physically, and that she couldn't wait to go home.

She threw a smile across to Zoltan, imagining his teeth gnashing together, relishing that thought. Thinking that the last thing he would have wanted was for her father to call, someone who would surely take her side in all of this.

Until there was a pause on the end of the line she could no longer ignore.

'Papa?'

The words she heard chilled her blood and made her dizzy with shock and disbelief. 'But, Papa, I do not understand.' And this time he said the words slower, so there could be no mistake, so she could not misunderstand.

'Aisha, you are not going home. Why has no-one told you yet? *You must marry Zoltan.*'

She made the mistake of looking up, caught the suddenly smug look on Zoltan's face, as if he had caught the gist of her conversation and knew it was not in her favour. Then again, he had probably read her reaction on her face. She spun around, turning her back on him, hating his air of casual boredom, hating the sudden curve she'd witnessed on his lips.

Hating everything about him.

'But, Papa…' she pleaded into the receiver, curving her free hand around the mouthpiece, shielding the panic in her voice and cursing her impulse to let Zoltan stay in the room while she took the call. But she was not done yet. 'I don't *want* to marry him!'

He wanted to choke. Did she for one moment actually imagine that he actually wanted to marry her? Laughable. But it wasn't laughable. It was painful, really, having to listen to one half of a conversation when that half was clearly going so wrong.

There were plenty more 'but, Papa's, a fair sprinkling of 'but why?'s and a lot of time where she said nothing but listened to what her father was telling her before she tried to get a word in. He had to admit the one that almost plucked at his heart strings was the 'Please, Papa, please!'

Said in her Poor Little Princess voice, it was quite touching, really. If you cared.

Even if you did, what could anyone do? Hadn't he explored every option himself?

But then the final cruncher—the 'Yes, Papa,' in a voice that sounded like a child's who had just been rebuked and told to be good—before she turned back to the desk and put the receiver down.

It was awkward witnessing someone else's humiliation, especially after they'd insisted you stayed and had acted as if it was going to be some kind of victory for them.

Awkward and yet, at the same time, supremely satisfying.

She didn't look up at him, but she didn't have to for him to realise she'd been crying. Her long lashes were clumped into thick black spikes, moisture glazed her eyes and he had to wonder why she insisted on making it so difficult for herself.

He'd learned early in life that some things were worth fighting for and some things were a lost cause from day one. 'Choose your battles,' his uncle, the King, had told him when he was just a young boy and still steaming after his father had, as usual, accepted Mustafa's side in a dispute. 'Don't waste your time on the things you can't change. Save your energy for the battles that count.'

He hadn't really understood the message back then; it had all just seemed so unfair that his father had never taken his word, no matter the truth of the matter. But bit by bit he'd learned that nothing would ever change and that arguing only made things worse.

Gradually he'd learned to accept the inevitable and save his energies for the battles he could win.

Someone should have told this woman the same thing.

Didn't she see there was no changing this? She was stuck. As stuck as he was in this centuries-old time warp. There was no getting out of it. There was no escape.

'So you managed to sort it all out?' he asked when she had stood there, her hands on the replaced receiver, for way too long.

She drew in a long breath then, blinked, straightened and made the tiniest concession she could to her tears by flicking them from the corners of her eye while making out as though she was pushing the weight of her long, dark hair back behind her ears.

'My father will be here tomorrow, as you said.' Her voice was low and flat, as if all the stuffing had been knocked out of it, all the life.

He waited longer still, struck by how much this admission of defeat cost her in her too-stiff spine and forced control, almost—if he had to admit it—admiring her. Maybe she wasn't as fragile as he had supposed or she would have been wailing on the end of the phone, dissolved into shrieks and fits of tears by now. Facing him after the instruction to stay, only for it to mean he had witnessed her humiliation, would be no easy task. Not for anyone, let alone some brittle, spoilt princess.

She blinked then as she looked up at him. 'My father—Sheikh Ashar—says I have no choice. Apparently neither of us do. It seems it is more complicated than a mere alliance. He says our countries are inexorably linked and that if this marriage doesn't happen both of our families forfeit their right to their respective thrones. So, if I say no, it will not only be Al-Jirad without a king.'

He waited. He had known this to be the truth, but she would never have believed him if he had told her. It was better coming from her father.

'So then, it is settled. There is no escaping this marriage, for either of us.'

She blinked up at him, her eyes as empty as her voice. 'Not unless I wish my father to lose the crown and my brothers to lose their birthright.'

She drew in breath and seemed to grow taller then, her chin raised, her eyes resigned but still, he noted, with a glimmer of defiance, even if still glassy. 'I would not do that to my family, of course.'

'Of course.'

'In which case, it seems there is no choice. Apparently I am stuck with this marriage.' Her chin grew higher then, her eyes grew colder, with an icy surface you could skate over. 'And so, it would seem, stuck with you.'

He watched her leave, her head held high, her posture impossibly straight and regal.

Haughtiness becomes you, he thought as she swept from the room, back to her princessly best, if you didn't count the riotous freefall of her hair tumbling down her back, hair that had felt like a silk curtain in his hands. He remembered the feel of her in his arms, the heat from her mouth, the softness and suppleness of her body against his, and he growled low and deep in his throat.

For all her protests, for all her pretence, there was a live woman under that haughty exterior, hot and wanting, and he would take great pleasure in peeling that harsh shell away piece by inevitable piece.

'What happened to you?' There was laughter in Rashid's words as he led the other two friends into the library and caught sight of Zoltan's cheek.

'Let me guess,' Bahir said with a knowing grin. 'The princess happened to him.'

Kadar perched himself on the edge of the desk where Zoltan sat and studied the three lines down his friend's cheek. 'No wonder she wasn't impressed by my fireworks. Looks like she's packing her own.'

Zoltan leaned back in his chair, pinching the bridge of his nose with his fingers, his head full of ancient verse after hours of study. No surprise that his friends would find this intensely amusing. They would no doubt find it doubly so if they knew exactly what he had been doing right before she had raked her claws down his cheek.

'I'm glad you all find this so entertaining. What are you doing here anyway? I thought you were falconing today.'

'We thought you might be lonely,' Rashid said, picking up a paperweight from the table and tossing it from one hand to the other. 'Didn't realise you were otherwise occupied.'

'Don't drop that,' Zoltan warned, thankful for the opportunity to change the subject. 'It's Murano glass, three-hundred years old. A present from the then-king to his sheikha. Worth a fortune, apparently.'

Bahir stopped tossing the paperweight for a moment, peering into the colours of its mysterious depths. 'Oh well,' he said, tossing it in Rashid's direction. 'Easy come, easy go.'

Kadar spun around the heavy tome sitting in front of Zoltan and peered down. 'What's this?'

'The Sacred Book of Al-Jirad. I have to know it by the coronation.'

'What? All of it?'

'The entire thing, chapter and verse. Ready to be quoted from at the appropriate moment, to spout the wisdom of the ages.'

Rashid whistled. 'Then, brother, you really do need rescuing.'

Kadar slammed the book shut before Zoltan could stop him. 'Come on, then,' he said, jumping to his feet.

'I don't have time,' he growled. 'I'll see you at dinner.'

'What, you're too busy to spend a few minutes with your best friends when we've all come so far to help you? Nice one.'

'Lame,' Rashid agreed, tossing the paperweight casually in one hand. 'Besides, you have to exercise some time. We're heading for the pool.' And he threw the paperweight at Zoltan so fast he almost fumbled the catch and dropped it to the marble floor.

'Reflexes a bit slow today?' he teased, looking at his cheek. Zoltan knew he wasn't talking about the paperweight. 'I reckon I might actually beat you over twenty laps today. What do you say?'

Zoltan was already on his feet. 'Not a chance.'

Aisha could not believe it had come to this. She lay on the big, soft bed, her pillows drenched with tears. But now, hours after she had returned from that fateful meeting in the library, her tears were spent, her eyes sore and scratchy, and she was left with just the aching chasm in her gut where hope had once resided.

There was no hope now. There was nothing but a yawning pit of despair from which she could see no way out.

For tomorrow she was required to marry Zoltan, an

arrogant, selfish, impossible man who clearly thought
her no more than a spoilt princess and who had made
it plain he considered she was getting the better end of
the deal in having to marry a barbarian like him, and
that there was not a thing she could do to avoid it. To re-
nege on the deal would result in bringing down the royal
families of two countries and smashing apart the alliance that had kept their countries strong for centuries.

And, for all the power that knowledge should bestow
upon her—that she was the king-maker of two countries—she had never felt more powerless in her life.

She had never felt more alone.

She rolled over on the bed, caught a glimpse in the
corner of her eye of the magnificent golden wedding-
robe sitting ready and waiting on a mannequin in the
corner of her room and squeezed her eyes shut again.

Such a beautiful gown. Such a work of art. *Such a
waste.* A gown like that deserved to be worn to a fairy-
tale wedding, whereas she was to be married to a monster. Expected to bear his sons, destined to be some
kind of brood mare. Doomed to never find the love for
which she had once hoped.

Such foolish dreams and hopes.

After all, she was a princess. She swiped at her
cheeks. What right had she had to wish for any kind
of normal life, even if her two brothers had the future
crown of Jemeya well and truly covered?

Yet still, other princes and princesses around the
world seemed to marry for love these days. Why
shouldn't she have dared hope for the same?

She shook her head. It was pointless feeling sorry
for herself. She forced herself to move, found herself a
wash cloth in the bathroom to run cold water over and
held it to her swollen, salt-crusted eyes. She could mope

for ever and it would not change things. Nothing she could do, it seemed, could change things.

She returned to her room, passing by the open balcony doors when the curtains shifted on a slight breeze as she still held the cool, soothing flannel to her cheeks. Rani must have opened them, she guessed, before she had left her to her despair, for she was sure the doors had not been open before.

Poor Rani. She had been so excited to show her the gown when she'd returned from her meeting with Zoltan, so delighted to tell her what was planned for her preparations the next day—the fragrant oil-baths, the henna and the hairdresser. Aisha had taken such strides to hold herself together until then, all the way from the library through the convoluted passageways and along the cloistered walk to her suite. It had been so much effort to hold herself together that, in spite of all of the young girl's enthusiasm—or maybe, in part, because of it—she had taken one look at the dress, collapsed onto the bed in tears and told the girl to go away.

The breeze from the open doors beckoned her, carrying with it the late-afternoon perfume of the garden below, the heady scent of jasmine and the sweet lure of orange blossom. It drew her to the window, to where the soft inner drapes danced and played upon the gentle breeze. She stood there for a moment before venturing out onto the balcony of her suite. The sun was dipping lower now, the evening rays turning the stone and roof of the palace gold, even in the places it was not. The garden was bathed in half-light, the sound of the splashing fountain and birdcalls coming from its green depths like an antidote to stress.

It all looked so restful and beautiful, so perfect, even

when she knew things were far from perfect, that she could not resist the lure of the perfumed garden.

A set of stairs led down from the balcony. She looked back into her suite and realised someone had already taken away the jacket she had torn off and discarded en route to her bed, but it didn't matter, because she probably wouldn't need it anyway. It was deliciously warm and without the sting of the sun's rays. It wasn't as though she was planning on running into anyone.

She wasn't in the mood for running into anyone. A lifetime of training had told her that she must be presentable at all times, in all situations, prepared for every contingency; given a lifetime of doing exactly that, only to find that your life could take a bizarre turn and force you into marriage with someone just because some crusty old piece of paper said you must, what then did it matter how she looked? She finger-combed her hair back from her face and smoothed her creased trousers with her hands. That would do. Once, she might have cared, but today, after all that had happened, she felt a strange sense of detachment from her former life.

It didn't matter any more.

If she could be married to someone she hated because the ancient alliance between their two countries dictated it, then nothing mattered any more—not how you looked, how you acted or certainly not what you dreamed and wanted from your life. Only that you were a princess. Only that you came from the right breeding stock. And Zoltan hated her anyway. It wasn't as though he cared how she looked.

Zoltan was stuck with her, just as she was stuck with him, and somehow that thought was vaguely comforting as she descended the stairs into the garden. After all, why should she be the only one inconvenienced by this arrangement? Why should she be the only one to suffer?

Her legs brushed past lavender bushes intruding onto the path as she walked, releasing their scent onto the air. She breathed deeply, taking it in, wishing herself the soothing balm it promised.

The garden was deserted, as she had hoped it would be, silent but for the rustle of leaves on the breeze, the play of water and the call of birds. She drifted aimlessly along its paths, breathing in the scented air, delighting in the discovery of the ever-changing view and the skillful placement of a bubbling bird-bath or a flowering frangipani to surprise and delight. She stopped by one such frangipani tree laden with richly scented flowers, picked a cluster of bright white-and-yellow flowers to her face and drank in their sweet perfume.

Her mother's favourite flower, so her father had told her when she had leafed through her parents' wedding photos. She could see her parents' wedding photos now, and her mother's bouquet, all tight white rosebuds amidst the happy brightness of frangipani flowers as she drank in that sweet scent.

She wondered what her mother would tell her now. Would she be as cold and clinical as her father, who had told her today that there was no point thinking or dreaming or wishing for things to be different, because she was what she was and that was how it was to be? Or would she be more understanding, at least empathetic of her situation?

And not for the first time she wondered about her own parents' marriage, wishing she knew more of the circumstances of how they had met. But her mother had died way too early for her to be interested in any of that, and now it was all so long ago.

She arrived at an opening in a wall, keyhole-shaped, potted palms on either side. A path to another garden? she wondered. But as she looked through it she could see it was not one but a series of archways through which she caught a glimpse of greenery and whispering palms that beckoned to her.

She looked back, trying to get her bearings so she would not get lost, saw what must be her balcony above the tangle of vegetation and realised she was in the far corner of the square, the other side of the palace to where the library lay.

Further from Zoltan, she figured, so maybe it wouldn't hurt to venture a little further, especially not if this was to be her new home.

She encountered only one other person, a maid, who blinked up at her, bowed and soundlessly and quickly moved on.

She passed by a bird-bath with a bubbling fountain where birds splashed happily, oblivious to her passing, and the breeze whispered through the palms, the promise of the archways luring her on. She loved them all. Every one of them was decorated slightly differently, one whose walls were covered with blue-and-white mosaic, another inlaid with mother-of-pearl, the last with a pair of peacocks with bright and colourful plumage, every one of them a work of art.

It was as she passed beneath that last richly decorated arch and wondered what she would find beyond that she heard it, a voice, a shout, and then splashing and laughter. *Men's laughter*, coming from some kind of pool. She swallowed as she swung around, pressing her back hard against the cool, tiled wall, grateful she had heard their voices before stumbling unknow-

ingly into their midst. She should not be here. She had
come too far.

And then she heard his voice amongst the others,
Zoltan's, and the bitter taste of bile rose in her throat
as she remembered how supremely difficult it had been
to walk from that library with her back straight and her
head held high when all she had felt like doing was col-
lapsing in a heap in despair—how it had taken every
shred of her self-control to force herself to wait until
she had walked through the door of her suite before
she could let her tears go. She could not bear to see
him again with those memories so vivid in her mind.

His voice rang out again, issuing some kind of challenge. There were calls and laughter, and the challenge
seemed to be accepted by another. The unfairness of it
all grated on her raw nerves, rubbed salt into her still-
fresh wounds. Clearly Zoltan was not agonising too
much over the stress of a forced marriage, for all his
protests about not wanting to take a wife. Clearly he was
not suffering unduly, if he could take time out to frolic
in a pool with his friends without a care in the world.
And clearly he had not felt the need to cry his heart
out on his bed at the unfairness of it all. The truth of it
struck home again. She was nothing in this world but
a pawn in a game where she didn't even merit a move.

There came a splash then, the sound of thrashing
water and cheers, and curiosity got the better of her.
Who were these men with Zoltan? Could they be the
ones who had accompanied him to the desert encampment last night? Maybe she could take one look. It
wasn't as though the pool was private; there was no
gate and she was simply out walking.

Making sure she stayed in the shadows under the

archway, she peered out past the garden surrounding the
pool. There were two men there, neither of them Zoltan,
standing cheering at the far end of a broad sapphire
pool, partly shaded by twin lines of palms. Though it
was nowhere near shady enough to hide the scars that
marred one man's back, the skin twisted and brutal-
looking, and she wondered what could have caused such
a mess as the water of the pool was torn apart by churn-
ing arms, going stroke for stroke as two more men de-
voured the length of the pool.

Until they reached the end and the water erupted as
someone emerged, using powerful arms to springboard
out a mere head before his rival.

'I win,' the first said, offering his hand to the second.

Zoltan, she realised, disappointed as her eyes drank
in the sight of him dripping wet. How typical that he
should win the race. How unfortunate. She would have
loved to see him lose. She would love to see something
or someone wipe that smug look of superiority off his
face and the sheer arrogance that infused every part of
his body, every glistening muscle, every hard-packed
limb.

Of course he would not have an ounce of fat on him,
she thought with added resentment, he would not allow
such a thing. She had seen enough. And she almost
managed to turn away until he flexed his shoulders as
her eyes caught the play of muscles under broad shoulders and tracked down the vee of his torso, to where
his hips were encased in black lycra above the start of
those long, powerful legs.

She sniffed, refusing to be impressed. So maybe she
had been wrong before. Maybe he was not *exactly* like
Mustafa, at least not in this one respect, she thought
as she remembered the fat man scratching the bulging

of his gut through his robe with long, almost feminine fingernails ending fingers adorned with gaudy rings. She shuddered, knowing how close she had come to that repulsive fate.

Still, it made no difference to her how many muscles Zoltan had, and she did not care that his skin glistened a golden-olive in the light. Not when in essence he was exactly the same as his half-brother. Not when there were still so very many reasons to hate him with every fibre of her being.

And she was sure, with time, she would find more.

'I gave you a head start,' his vanquished rival claimed as she watched furtively from the shadows. 'Let's make it best out of three.' Zoltan laughed and slapped his friend on the back, turning his face to the sky to shake the water from his dark hair. She had to blink and look again to make sure it was him.

Zoltan actually laughed? Was this the same man as the monster she had met today in the library? Was this the dark barbarian who had snarled and growled and so smugly informed her that she had no choice? For when he smiled, when he laughed so openly, his face was transformed. Not handsome, exactly. He would never be handsome. His face was too dark, his features too strong, like the strongest, bitterest cup of coffee imaginable. But with laughter lighting his dark features he almost looked human.

Almost—*good*.

Electricity sizzled down her spine and her mouth turned ashen. Tomorrow—*tomorrow*—this man would be her husband. This hated man would lie next to her in bed, wearing even less than he was wearing now. And expecting her...

She shivered, feeling a growing apprehension that the unknown would soon become known.

She clutched the flowers in her hands to her face, burying herself in their fragrant scent.

This was not how she had imagined it would be.

'Princess Aisha?'

CHAPTER FIVE

THE flowers fell from her hand as she turned, the vizier behind her bowing respectfully. 'One of the maids saw you walking. Is there something in particular you were looking for, Princess?' He glanced across at the pool, and she followed his gaze to where all four men were now gathered at the near end, laughing together, all four of them bronzed and built, with strong masculine features, all of them impressive in their own way. Once again she wondered whether they might be the same men who had helped pluck her from Mustafa last night. Her gaze returned to the enigma that was Zoltan. There was something about him that set him apart and that caused her pulse to trip. 'You are a long way from your suite.'

She turned to see him watching her. 'I was enchanted by the garden,' she said, her cheeks blazing with embarrassment at being caught peering covertly from the shadows and now openly staring. 'I did not know where the path would lead me. I was about to head back.'

He nodded. 'Rani has brought your meal. Perhaps you would permit me to show you back to your suite?' he said, and she knew it wasn't a question. She also knew she wasn't about to refuse.

'Of course,' she said, wanting to be as far away from

the mystery that was Zoltan—the laughing barbarian with the gleaming skin, the man who would be her husband tomorrow—as she could get.

'Princess!'

Too late.

She felt his call in a searing sizzle of heat down her spine, guilt-stricken that she had been discovered, a voyeur in the shadows, and not only by the vizier but now by Zoltan himself.

She wondered how much humiliation it was humanly possible to suffer in one day, for right now, the supply seemed endless. And this time she had no-one to blame but her own wretched curiosity.

Would he be angry with her for spying on him? Or would he laugh at her, the way he did, with unsubtle jibes, mocking words and that unmistakable upturn of his lips?

Either way, she hated him all the more for it. And she hated her own stupid lack of judgement for not leaving the moment she had realised he was here. Hated that he made her feel so off-balance and uncertain. Hated that he so badly affected her judgement.

She dragged in the scented air as she turned, praying for strength, steeling herself for the confrontation.

But nothing could have prepared her for the full impact of that near-naked body approaching. Her mouth went dry, her heart rate doubled and kept right on going, and her eyes didn't know where to look. He was so big, his glistening golden-olive skin beaded with moisture, his chest sprinkled with black hair circling dark nipples before arrowing south, over a taut, hard-packed torso...

She dared not look too far south. Instead she focused on the white towel he had picked up and which he now used to pat his face dry as droplets continued to rain from the slicked-back tendrils of his hair. But the snowy whiteness of the towel only served to highlight the rich glow of his skin, to contrast against the darkness of his features, and would have been of much more help to her right now if he lashed it firmly around his waist.

'You should have brought your swimsuit if you wanted a swim,' he said, dismissing the vizier with a brief nod over her shoulder, before taking in the cool shell-top and her bare arms.

She realised he was not angry, as she had feared he might be, but was laughing at her again. Right now she would have preferred the anger.

'Unless of course,' he added, his dark eyes raking over her heated face, 'you prefer swimming *au naturel*?'

'No!' Her prissy-sounding outburst escaped before she could stop it, just as she could no more prevent her cheeks flushing with embarrassment. The thought of being any more exposed to his scrutiny than she already was made her skin tingle and goose bump. But the thought of being naked in the same pool with him triggered an entirely new and more potent kind of re- action. She could already imagine the feel of the water cool against her tight nipples, the pull of the water tug- ging at her curls as it slipped between her aching, heated thighs...

She squeezed her legs together, wishing to God she'd bothered to find her jacket so that he might not witness any more of her body's reaction to his presence, cross- ing her arms over her breasts so that they could not be- tray her. 'I was just going for a walk,' she said, her nails pressing into her arms, harder and deeper, while she wished fervently that he would use that damned towel and cover himself, if only so she was not so tempted to look *there*. 'To clear my head.'

'A good plan,' he conceded, dashing her hopes when he balled the towel in one fist and flung it to one side. *Yet another reason to hate him*, she told herself, for any reasonable man would surely cover himself up in front of a lady—*a princess*. But this was clearly no reasonable man. He was a barbarian who had treated her, and continued to treat her, appallingly. Definitely a barbarian, arrogant, self-assured and clearly used to parading near-naked around women. So what if he managed to look almost human when he smiled and when he laughed? He did not smile for her, he did not laugh with her.

This man laughed at her.

And she hated him for it.

She might have told him that too, but just then he reached down before her and picked up the flowers she had dropped and long forgotten. 'It is a good time to walk in the garden. All the evening flowers send out their perfume to sweeten our sleep and make us forget the heat of the day and let us dream of cooler seasons.' Then he held the floral sprigs to his nose, breathing in their heady scent, closing his eyes for a second, giving her the chance to study him more closely—his sooty lashes and brows, the strong blade of his nose and the three long, red marks left so unashamedly by her own raking nails. 'Beautiful,' he said, surprising her again. And then he looked across. 'Did you drop them?'

When she nodded, because her throat was suddenly too tight to speak, he gently tugged one of the flowers and slipped it into the tumble of her hair behind her ear, presenting her with the rest of the scented bouquet.

'I should go,' she said, taking them and already backing away, disturbed beyond measure by even just the brush of his fingers in her hair, the touch of his fingers against hers. She was unsettled by his proximity and how it put all of her senses on high alert. Confused by a man who suddenly seemed once more like her rescuer of last night, the man whose warm body she had huddled against, rather than the barbarian who had attacked her today and so mercilessly dismantled her defences.

How could a man she hated on such a fundamental level stir such feelings within her?

For this was the same man, she battled to remind herself, the same ruthless man who had only rescued her so he could be king. But of course he could afford to look more relaxed now. He had no need to argue with her because he had got what he had wanted. He knew that she had been forced into compliance with this marriage, that she knew she had no choice. He knew she wasn't going anywhere and that he had won.

He didn't want a wife.

He just wanted to be king. She just happened to be the one who could make it possible. She was merely the means to an end.

Oh yes, there was good reason why he could laugh and smile with his friends now and afford to be more civil to her, and that knowledge only served to fuel the burning hatred she felt for him. Because he assumed she was a done deal. He assumed that, once her father had told her straight, she would do what she was required to do without any more complaint and become his compliant bride.

Like hell.

And that thought gave her strength.

It gave her back the power to be herself. 'You are busy and I am interrupting,' she said. But when she looked over to the pool and scanned its surrounds for the proof to support her argument, she found it empty, the sapphire surface of the water unbroken, his friends nowhere to be seen. She frowned. How had they left and she not even noticed? For now she was alone here with him, with him wearing nothing more than a stretch of black lycra. She looked down at the flowers in her hand and swallowed, trying hard to focus on them and not let her gaze wander from the detail of their cleverly sculpted petals, the delicate curve, the subtle shading of colours. Anything that might stop her gaze or her focus from wandering further afield where she might catch a glimpse of his powerful legs or that bulging band of black lycra hinting at what lay below. 'I really have to go.'

'So you said.' He smiled, enjoying the start-again stop-again nature of her icy armour. For a moment she'd seemed to be regaining some composure, some of that haughtiness he'd witnessed in the library, but now once again she seemed unsure of herself, almost confused, like an actor having trouble staying in character.

How long had she been standing in the shadows watching? What had she been thinking that turned her cheeks such a deliciously guilty shade of red?

Whatever it was, she didn't look haughty now, like she had when she had marched so erect and cold from the library. She looked shy and vulnerable, a woman again, rather than an ice princess. A woman who didn't seem to know where to look.

'Is something wrong, Princess? You seem—agitated.'

She looked up at him then, her once kohl-rimmed eyes now a smudgy grey and overflowing with exasperation. 'You could cover yourself! I'm not used to talking to a near-naked man.'

'Only watching them, apparently,' he said, while secretly pleased to hear it. He didn't want to think of her with other men. She would have had them. God, she was nearly twenty-four—of course she would have had them. But at least, unlike her sister, she had chosen to be discreet about them.

'I didn't know you were here!'

'And when you did, you left immediately.' He was already reaching for the towel he'd flung down earlier. In one smooth movement he had it wrapped low around his hips and knotted it tight. He held his hands out by his sides. 'Is that better?'

'A little,' she said, though still her eyes skated away every chance they got. 'Thank you. And now I must go.'

'Stay a moment longer,' he said, enjoying his prickly princess too much to let her go just yet. She was a strange one, this one, moving through a range of emotions and reactions too fast for him to keep up with or to understand, frustrating him to hell because he didn't know what he was dealing with on the one hand, intriguing him on the other. 'There are some friends of mine you should meet. Or meet again, without their masks this time.' Then he glanced over his shoulder, wanting to call them over so that he could introduce them, surprised when he found they had disappeared without his noticing. More surprised that they were not already queued up to congratulate the woman who had left her mark on him not just once but twice in the space of twenty-four hours.

Maybe they had realised that this was his battle and his alone and it was better to leave him to it. Not that they wouldn't relish the opportunity to rub it in every chance they got.

But there would be time to introduce her to them tomorrow at the wedding and maybe by then the marks on his face and hand would have faded and they might have forgotten.

And maybe camels might grow wings and fly.

More likely they were just hoping that by tomorrow she might have added to his list of injuries.

'Your friends have gone,' she said. 'And so must I.'

On an impulse he didn't quite understand himself, but knowing his friends would understand a rapid change of plans, he almost asked her to dine with him.

Almost, except he stopped himself at the last moment. For the dinner he had planned with his friends would take no time at all, and then he would be back to his books and his study, which was where he needed to be if he was ever going to be prepared for the requirements of his new role.

Whereas dinner with this woman? Who knew where that would lead, given the startling turn events had taken today? He didn't even know how it had happened. But he did remember the feel of her in his arms, the way she'd turned so suddenly from a rigid column of shock to lush feminine need with just one heated, molten kiss. Would he be tempted to linger if he dined with her tonight, tempted to make her truly his before she became his bride? It made no difference to him.

But then he remembered the cold slash of her claws down his cheek.

He did not need another reminder of how much she objected to this marriage, certainly not before the wedding. And they would be married soon enough. She would be his tomorrow night in every sense of the word, and he could wait that long. He didn't need another battle at this stage, not when he had already won the war.

'Then good night, Princess,' he said with a bow.

'Sleep well. And when next we meet, it will be at our marriage.'

And he let her go. He watched her turn and walk purposefully away from him, watched the sway of her hips as she moved through the arched walkway to where Hamzah joined her to guide her back to her suite along the archway walk.

He turned away before she disappeared, cursing duty and all that came with it—the duty that forced him into this situation, the duty that insisted he marry this particular woman at this particular time, the duty that meant he would spend his night trying to memorize a crusty old book rather than burying himself in the body of a woman who looked and walked like a goddess. A woman who apparently hated the thought of doing her duty even more than he did.

Or maybe she just needed a bit more time to get used to the idea. That would make sense. He'd had three days since being informed of the disaster and what its implications were—that he should prepare himself for the fact he could be the one to inherit the throne. She'd had little more than that number in hours. And, even though her father had told her there was no other course of action, of course she would still be in denial, wanting to wish away her fate.

So maybe it was a good thing he had not asked her to dine with him. Because now she would have this night by herself, this one last night to enjoy her freedom.

And tomorrow, and for all the nights that would follow, her duty would be clear. Her duty would be with him.

In his bed.

CHAPTER SIX

'It is time, Princess.'

Startled, Aisha looked up from the cushioned seat where it seemed a hundred willing hands had been busy making the final adjustments to her veil and make-up until only a moment ago, whereas now she felt only the cold fingers of dread clawing at her insides. Surely it could not be time for the ceremony already? The day had passed in a blur of preparations, starting with a warm, oil-scented bath and moving on a seemingly never-ending conveyor-belt of sensual indulgences: a massage that had promised to soothe the tightness between her shoulders and yet had proved ultimately futile, before a facial, manicure and pedicure and the delicate, tickling touch of the henna artist creating golden swirling patterns on the backs of her hands and feet, a gesture of her acceptance of the Al-Jiradi ways.

It had all taken hours, yet surely it could not already be time? But the hands of the mantel clock offered no respite. Rani was right. The ceremony would begin in less than ten minutes.

She squeezed her eyes shut, feeling physically ill despite having barely eaten a thing all day.

'Do not be nervous, Princess,' reassured Rani. 'You look beautiful.' Clearly she mistook her reaction for normal pre-wedding jitters. But how could this be normal wedding nerves when most brides actually chose to get married? Or at least had a say in who they married. No, there was nothing normal about this marriage. Even if the mirror that Rani suddenly produced and held in front of her made her gasp.

She blinked, and looked again. Was that woman in the mirror, that woman adorned in golden robes, with her dark hair twisted with ropes of pearls and curled behind her head, really her? Her eyes looked enormous, rimmed with kohl and shimmering with glitter, her lips plumped and gloss-slicked ruby red. She looked every bit a real bride.

The enormity of what she was being forced into was like a lead weight on her chest. Married to a stranger. A despot.

A barbarian who cared nothing for her, but only what she could do for him.

What a waste it had been, feeling relief at escaping from Mustafa's slimy-fingered clutches, for here she was, being forced to marry yet another arrogant captor.

One of the other women tinkered with the fall of her veil, while Rani searched her face for any flaws. 'You look perfect, Princess. Sheikh Zoltan will not be able to resist his new wife.'

Oh hell! She jammed her lips shut. It was either that or bolt for the bathroom, with metres of golden embroidered silks fluttering in her wake, to throw up the few sips of sweet tea she had managed to swallow.

She clamped her eyes shut and concentrated, swallowing down on the urge, concentrating on her breathing. She would not let that happen. She was a princess of Jemeya, after all. She would not shame her father or her country in such a fashion.

Instead she willed her body to calm until she was back in control again, smiled the best she could at the waiting group of women all glowing with satisfaction with the results of their handiwork, and said with only a hint of irony, 'Then we must not keep Sheikh Zoltan waiting.'

It was to be a brief affair—just a small gathering, she had been advised—in deference to the recent demise of the royal family, which was the reason why it was being held here at this palace rather than the Blue Palace. The actual coronation would be held there in a few more days after the traditional mourning period, but his wedding now would cement Zoltan as the next king.

The ceremony itself was painfully brief. Her stomach still in knots, she was led slowly to a gilded ballroom where both her father and Zoltan stood waiting for her at the front of a small gathering of guests and officials, already seated at low tables for the feasting to follow. She searched the faces looking at her but failed to find her sister amongst them and felt a bubble of disappointment that she hadn't bothered or been able to attend. But that was her sister and it was half of why she loved her so much. Instead of following convention and trying to do the right thing, Marina made her own rules and lived by them, and she didn't blame anyone else when they went wrong.

Maybe her sister had been right all along.

The attendees fell silent and rose as one as she arrived, and to the sound of music, the beat of drums, the stringed oud and the haunting ney reed pipe, she moved across the room and forward to her fate. Her father nodded and beamed at her approvingly, partly, she knew, the smile of a man who had not seen his daughter for a few days, but also the smile of a man who would keep his crown. And she could not find fault with him for that. He had been born to be king. He knew nothing else. Jemeya knew no other way.

Besides, he was her father and she loved him, and so she did her best to warm her frozen face and smile back, not sure whether she had succeeded.

The other man stood a good head taller, and she almost missed her step when she saw the evidence of her nails still clear on his cheek. She lifted her gaze higher, saw his dark, assessing eyes on her, and felt an instantaneous rush of heat blossom in her bones and suffuse her flesh with what she saw there.

Oh, there was still the resentment, hard-edged and critical and matching the unrelenting set of his jaw. There was still the smug satisfaction at achieving what he had set out to do in order to become king. But it was the savage heat she saw burning inside those eyes that started fires under her own skin. A savage desire.

For her.

Her gaze dropped to the floor as she took those final, fateful steps. She could not breathe. Could barely think. Was only half-aware as the music ceased except for the drumming, only to realise it was her own heartbeat she was hearing. And then someone—the vizier?—uttered something and took her hennaed right hand and placed it in her father's palm. After barely a handful more words, her wrist was lifted and passed to Zoltan's waiting hand and, as easily as that, it was done. She was married.

Somewhere outside a cannon boomed, while inside the music resumed, brighter now and faster, signalling the end of the formalities and the start of the wedding celebrations and the feasting to come, but the music washed over her; her father's congratulations washed over her.

She was married.

They were led to their seats. She went as if in a daze, and all the time Zoltan kept hold of her hand, his warm fingers wound tightly around hers, almost as if he feared she would run if he let go. Foolish man. He should know there was nowhere for her to run now.

There was no escape.

She was married.

But she would not look at him, afraid that if she did she might once again witness that burning need and feel that potent reaction in her own body.

His thumb stroked her hand and she squeezed her eyes shut, trying to stop the warmth from his touch coursing up her arm. Why did he do that?

She did not want to feel this way. She hated him. She must not feel that way. And yet still her flesh tingled and burned, her breasts felt plumped and heavy and her thighs bore an unfamiliar ache…

It was not fair. And while she grappled with the reactions of a traitorous body, she was barely aware of the staff descending from every direction, filling glasses and delivering steaming platters until the table was sagging under the weight of food that she knew must smell wonderful and taste delicious. But she smelt nothing, could bring herself to taste nothing.

'Perhaps you might smile,' Zoltan leaned close to say.

Through the fog of her senses, she heard the bite in his voice, the rebuke, and it woke her from her stupor. This was Zoltan next to her, the barbarian sheikh. If she had witnessed need in his eyes, it was the need to possess her to take the crown of Al-Jirad. That was what she had witnessed in those greedy eyes. Nothing more.

She pulled her hand from his and used it to reach for her water so he could not take it back and stir her senses with the gentle stroke of his thumb again. 'Perhaps I do not find reason to smile.'

'This is our wedding day.'

She glared at him then, allowed her eyes to convey all the resentment and hatred she had for him and for being forced into this position. 'Precisely!' she hissed. 'So it is not like there is anything to smile about.'

A muscle in his jaw popped. His eyes were as cold and flat as a slab of marble, and she knew at that moment he hated her, and she was glad. There would be no more hand stroking if she could help it.

She sipped her water, celebrating her good fortune, but her success and his fury were short-lived, his features softening at the edges as he scooped up a ripe peach from a tray of fruit. 'Oh, I don't know,' he said, running his fingers over the velvet skin of the peach almost as if he was caressing it, holding it to his face to breathe in its fresh, sweet scent. 'There's always the anticipation of one's wedding night to bring a smile to one's face, wouldn't you say?'

And he bit deeply into the flesh of the peach, juice running down his chin, his eyes fixed on hers. Challenging. *Mocking.*

'You're disgusting!' she said, already rising to leave, unable to stand being alongside him a moment longer.

'And you,' he said, grabbing hold of her wrist, the corners of his lips turning up, 'are my sheikha. Do not forget that.'

'What hope is there of that?'

'None at all, if I have anything to do with it. Now sit down and smile. You are attracting attention.'

She looked around and saw heads turned her way,

the faces half openly curious, the other half frowning, except for the three men who sat at a table nearby who looked to be almost enjoying the show, the same men who had been with Zoltan last evening at the pool.

'Who are those men?' she asked, sitting down to quell curiosity and deflect attention from herself rather than because she wanted to, determined not to accede to his demand quietly. It worked. People soon returned to the feast and to the conversation.

'Which men?'

'The three you were with last night,' she said, rubbing her wrist where he had held her, damning a touch which seemed to leave a burning memory seared on her flesh. 'The ones sitting over there looking like the falcons that caught the hare.'

He knew who she was referring to before he followed her gaze to see his three friends sat talking amongst themselves, openly amused by the proceedings. 'They are friends of mine.'

'Are they the ones who were with you the night you came to Mustafa's camp?'

He looked back at her, amused by her choice of words. 'You mean the night we rescued you?' The glare he earned back in response was worth it. 'Yes, they are the ones. On the left is Bahir, in the centre, Rashid, and the one on the right is Kadar.'

Her eyes narrowed. 'He is the one with the scar on his back?'

'That is him.'

He waited for her to ask for details, like most women he knew would, but instead she just nodded, surprising him by asking, 'And you are the only one married?'

'As of today.'

'Why?'

'What do you mean, "why"?'

Alongside him she shrugged and took a sip from her glass of water, taking her own sweet time to answer. 'Oh, I don't know. I see three men who are clearly of marriageable age and who all look fairly decent with their clothes off. Your friends are all—what is that expression they use in women's magazines?—ripped?'

Her words trailed off, leaving him to deal with the uncomfortable knowledge that she thought his friends looked good with their clothes off, his gut squeezing tight in response. He didn't like that. He didn't want her looking at them. He looked over to where the trio sat, knowing that if they only knew they would never let him live it down.

'And of course,' she continued, 'you all seem quite friendly.'

'What's that supposed to mean?' he said, already suspecting where this was going.

For the first time she chose to look directly at him, rather than choosing to avert her eyes. She arched one eyebrow high, her eyes brimming with feigned innocence. 'Naturally, I was wondering, maybe you're all gay or something? Not that that's a problem, per se, you understand. But it would explain why none of you have wives or women.'

He could not believe what he was hearing. If they had been anywhere else... If they had been anywhere but sitting in the midst of a crowded room where they were the centre of attention, he would have rucked up her golden skirts and shown her just how far from gay he was right here and now.

But he did not have to resort to such means, not given their eventful, albeit brief, history. She could not have forgotten already. 'I seem to recall a certain incident in the library yesterday. I seem to recall you being there. Do you really have cause to wonder if I am gay?'

She shrugged again and picked a grape from a bunch, the first item of food he'd seen her take. 'So maybe you swing both ways,' she said, her eyes outlined and as bold as that sharp tongue of hers. 'How am I supposed to know? After all, you were the one who said you never wanted a wife. And you are only marrying me so you can get the throne of Al-Jirad. What do you expect me to make of that?'

He growled, looking around at their guests, happy, loud and deep in the celebrations, and wondered if anyone would actually notice if he did drag her off to some sheltered alcove and put her concerns about his sexuality to bed this very minute. The thought made him stir, and not for the first time today. The moment she had walked into the ballroom, shrouded from head to toe in her golden wrapping, looking more like a goddess than any woman he had ever seen, he had lusted to peel each and every one of those robes and veils from her until she stood naked before him.

'Let me assure you,' he said, aware of three pairs of eyes studying them intently, judging their interaction, instead of watching the dancers like everyone else, no doubt hoping for more sparks to further entertain them. 'You need have no concerns on that score.

'And one more thing,' he added almost as an afterthought, when he noticed she was now making an entire course of grape number two. 'If I might suggest something?'

'What?'

'In the interests of allaying any and all concerns you have about my sexuality, you would be wise to eat something much more substantial. You're going to be needing your strength tonight.'

The grape went down the wrong way, the dancers finished, and it was only that the applause drowned out the sound of her coughing that hardly anyone realised she was choking.

Bastard!

Her father topped up her water but she was already on her feet, one of her attendants coming to help her manage her robes. 'Where are you going?' Zoltan demanded to know, rising to his feet beside her.

'The bathroom. Is that permitted, Your Arrogance?'

He let her go this time and she swept from the room, on the outside a cloud of sparkling gold, on the inside a raging black thundercloud.

She bypassed the bathroom, needing to stride the long corridors, needing to pound the flagstones in an effort to pound the man out of her psyche, until finally she stopped by an open window looking over yet another shady garden. She breathed deeply of the fragrant air, praying it lend her strength. She needed space. Space from that barbarian she was now wedded to. Space from the knowledge that tonight he would expect to make her his wife in every sense of the word.

And she was so very afraid.

She should never have goaded him. She should have known he would find a way to strike back at her, that her tiny victory would be only short-lived.

She looked up to see the vapour trail of a jet neatly bisecting the endless blue of the sky with a thin white line, the tiny plane no more than a diamond sparkling in the sun. She wished with all her heart that she were on that plane right now, flying as far, far away from

Al-Jirad, Zoltan and her birthright as she could possibly get.

But she was not, because she was a princess, and duty ordained that she do this thing, that she marry a man she didn't love.

Duty.

Such a little word. Such a huge impost. And tonight Zoltan would expect her to do her duty again and let him bed her.

She shuddered at the thought, suddenly assailed by myriad images and sensations cascading over her: the feel of his strong arms around her in the library, his hot mouth seeking hers, plundering hers, the sight of his body, fresh from his swim, the slide of droplets down his satin-skinned chest…

She breathed in the perfumed air and watched the tiny speck of a plane disappear into the distance as she thought of her shattered dreams and hopes. No hope of marrying a man she loved. No escape from a forced marriage. Not now.

But that did not mean she was completely powerless.

'Princess,' Rani said beside her, 'the Sheikh will be worried.'

She nodded as an idea formed and took shape in her mind, but knowing what Rani said to be true. Any moment Zoltan was sure to send out the storm troopers to find her and drag her back.

So there was no escape. She was stuck in this marriage with him. But Zoltan was a fool if he thought that meant he would have it all his own way and that she would deliver herself up to him on a platter.

She would not waste herself that way.

She had not saved herself all these years to be taken by a barbarian.

* * *

'What are you doing here?'

She stilled at the desk where she was sitting, pausing mid-sentence in the letter she was writing longhand to her sister to tell her about the wedding. In all likelihood it would never be sent, the details too baring, too revealing, but it was cathartic, writing it all down, putting her thoughts and shattered dreams into words.

But partly it had been something to pass the time, something to placate her mounting nerves, to do while waiting for the inevitable knock on the door.

She'd known that eventually he'd finish his drinks with his friends or whatever it was that he'd excused himself to do and that had kept him so long after the ceremony, wonder where she was and come looking for her. She should have known that he wouldn't wait for her to open the door to barge in, all aggrieved and affronted masculine pride.

She rose to face him, willing away the heat in her cheeks. Against Rani's shocked protests, she'd unwound herself from the metres and metres of golden fabric, pulled down her hair and scrubbed her face clean, dressing instead in a simple white nightdress, with a white robe lashed at her waist. Now only the henna tattoos adorning the backs of her hands and feet remained, but even they would fade in time and at least she no longer felt like some kind of prize to be fought and waged war over and dressed up like some kind of triumph. She felt like herself. Not even a princess any more, but a woman.

A woman with a mind of her own. A woman who knew about duty, but who also had her own hopes and dreams for the future.

That woman faced up to him now.

'Why wouldn't I be here?' She swallowed and tugged on the ends of her robe's ties, taking both mental and physical reinforcement from the action. 'After all, this is *my* suite, Sheikh Zoltan.' She put the emphasis squarely on the 'my'.

'And this is our wedding night!'

Packed with memories she would cherish for ever. What a laugh. She shrugged, realising she hadn't been the only one to divest of her wedding garb. He'd changed too out of that crisp, white wedding robe and into a pair of perfectly tailored trousers and a smooth fine-knit shirt that clung to his chest like a lover's caress. But no, she would rather not think of his lovers right now, or how many he must have had, or what their hands might do with a chest like that to explore. Not that she was jealous, exactly. It was just that she did not care to know the details.

She lifted her gaze to his face, plastering a disingenuous expression on her own. 'Your point being?'

'You are supposed to be in my chamber. Didn't they tell you I was expecting to find you in my suite?'

She sniffed, looking down at the desk and fingering the hand-written pages, thinking about all the things she'd talked about, all her hopes and her disappointments, exposing herself and her pointless dreams. No, she probably wouldn't end up sending it, come to think of it. Her seize-the-moment sister would probably only laugh and say that no man was worth waiting for, especially the one you didn't even know existed. She looked back up at Zoltan, waiting like a mountain before her. 'I do believe someone mentioned something like that, yes.'

'Then why did I have to come looking for you here?'

'Because there seemed no point in going to your room.'

He raked one hand through his hair. 'What the hell

are you talking about? Why not, when you knew I had been expecting to find you there?'

'Simply because I thought it might give you the wrong idea,' she said, pausing to enjoy the mess of confusion on his features and the questions flashing across his eyes before deciding to put him out of his misery. 'Given the fact I have no intention of sleeping with you.'

CHAPTER SEVEN

THE mountain before her turned volcanic, the face glowing hot with the magma so close below the surface, eyes wild. She braced herself for the eruption, knowing she was courting disaster and yet feeling a strange sense of elation that she'd succeeded in throwing him so completely off-balance. But the expected eruption did not eventuate. Zoltan somehow managed to hold himself together, his rage rolling off him in searing waves of heat. 'Is this some kind of joke?'

'Rest assured, Sheikh Zoltan,' she said, aiming for meekness. 'I would never joke about such a thing. I am deadly serious.'

'But you are my *wife*!' he roared, rigid with fury. 'Let me remind you of that fact, in case today's ceremony had somehow slipped your mind.'

This time she could not help but laugh. 'Do you seriously think for a moment I could forget, when I was handed over to you like little more than a stick of furniture?'

'Oh,' he said, pacing out the width of the Persian rug that took up one half of the room before turning to devour the distance back in long, purposeful strides, his thumb stroking his chin as if he were deep in contemplation of some highly complex problem. 'I see your problem. You think it should have been all about you, the poor little princess forced to do her duty for once in her life? Do you think we should have got down on hands and bended knees and thanked you for so generously sacrificing yourself on the altar of martyrdom? For so generously agreeing to do what was your duty?'

She closed her eyes as she took a despairing breath, ignoring his barbs and insults except to use them to fuel her resolve. If she had a problem, it was standing not ten feet from her. 'No, I don't think that at all. For, while I'm not overly fond of finding myself a pawn in someone else's game—a game, it seems, where I find myself a loser from the very beginning—I actually don't think I'm the one with the problem here.

'You needed a wife—a princess, no less—in order to be king and today you got one. So now you can be crowned King of Al-Jirad. You have my heartiest congratulations.' She looked towards the door 'And now, if you wouldn't mind leaving, Sheikh Zoltan, I will finish my correspondence.'

He stood, slowly shaking his head. 'You are kidding yourself if you think that, Princess. You think this ends here? You know Al-Jirad needs an heir. Two at least before your work is anywhere near done.'

She angled her chin higher. 'I acknowledge that my services are also required as some kind of brood mare. I do not particularly like it, but I accept that it is so.'

His eyes gleamed in the light. 'Then what are you doing here and not already in my suite?'

'Simple,' she said, crossing her arms over her chest, refusing to be cowed. 'I don't know you. I won't sleep with a man I don't know, whoever he is, whether or not he believes he has some kind of legal entitlement to my breeding services.'

He came closer then, so close she could feel the air shift and curl between them, carrying his scent to her on a heated wave. It was all she could do to stand her ground and not turn and run, and only half from fear of his anger. The other half was from fear that, in spite of her anger and her hatred for him, she might yet be drawn towards an evocative scent that brought back memories of lying wrapped in his arms, close to his heated body.

She swallowed as he came close. But surely he would not try anything here, in her suite? Surely he was not that ruthless that he could come here to take what she had denied him elsewhere?

'You don't know me, Princess?' He scooped the back of one finger down her cheek, an electric, evocative gesture that sent ripples of sensation radiating out under her skin. 'Not at all?'

'No,' she said, hating it when he slid his hand around the curve of her throat. 'I know practically nothing about you.' She willed herself to be strong, to remember his cruelty and the fact he was using her, even as her skin tingled, her traitorous body yearning to sway into his touch. 'And to tell you the truth, I'm not particularly fond of the bits I have seen.'

'Strange,' he mused. 'When I had been sure there was a definite connection between us.' He angled his head. 'Did you not feel it then, when we kissed?'

'I felt nothing but revulsion!'

'Then I am mistaken. It must have been your sensual twin sister in my arms in that library. That woman was warm and willing and had a fire raging inside her that I longed to quench.'

She spun away, discomfited by his words. Shamed

by the parts that hit too close to home. 'You are very much mistaken!'

He stood there where she had left him like a dark thundercloud. 'It is you who is mistaken, Princess, thinking you have a choice about this, barricading yourself away in your room like some kind of virginal nun seeking sanctuary when you should already be on your back working to provide Al-Jirad with the heirs it requires.'

Her blood simmered and spat, turned molten in her veins and seared its way under her skin. It was all she could do to swallow back on the bitter bile that ached to infuse her words. 'How tempting you make it sound, Sheikh Zoltan. You paint a picture in which any woman would be mad not to want a starring role—on her back, ready to be serviced by the barbarian sheikh!'

She turned away, unable to look at him a moment longer, unable to banish the unwelcome pictures in her mind's eye—and the unwelcome rush of heat that had accompanied them—needing air and space and everything she knew she would never find in this marriage where she was stuck with him for ever.

A hand clamped down on her shoulder and wrenched her around. 'What did you call me?'

She looked purposefully down at his hand on her arm, and then up to him. 'Only what you are. A barbarian.'

He smiled then, if you could call it that, baring his teeth like a wild animal before it lunges for the kill, his eyes alert and anticipating her every move. Her simmering blood spun faster and more frantic in her veins.

'I seem to recall you calling me a barbarian once before, Princess,' he said, tugging her closer, sliding his free hand down her arm, and then so slowly up

again. 'Maybe you are right. Maybe I am only a barbarian—the princess's personal barbarian. Do you like the
sound of that? Would that excite you? Does it heat your
blood like it did yesterday in the library?' He looked
past her shoulder to the massive, wide bed that lay so
broad and inviting across the room, and when he looked
back at her his eyes gleamed with purpose. 'Is that why
you stayed here in your room?' He looked down at the
simple robe she was wearing, flicking the collar under
his thumb, and she could tell he was working out how
easy it would be to discard. 'Is that why you changed
out of your wedding gown, so that when I came and got
angry, as you knew I must, it would be no challenge to
tear off your robe and gown and bare you to my gaze?'

'You kid yourself,' she whispered, her breath coming rapid and shallow. She hated what he was doing to
her body, hated herself for imagining the scene he por-
trayed and for wondering what it would be like to be
taken by one so powerful. And she felt confused and
conflicted—she hated him, and he was being a monster,
yet still heat mounted inside her, still the excitement of
his touch and his words tugged and awoke some deeply
buried carnal self.

'Do I?' He touched the pad of his thumb to her parted
lips, and she trembled and saw his answering smile
when she did. 'For, given that I am a barbarian, I could
take you now and save myself the trouble of carrying
you all the way to my suite.'

His predatory smile widened. He stepped in closer,
let go his grip on her arm and used both his hands to
scoop behind her neck and into her scalp, under the
weight of her thick black hair. 'Would you like that,
Princess?'

She swallowed, having to put up her hands against

his hard chest to stop herself from falling into him. 'You wouldn't dare.' But she wouldn't bet on it.

'And maybe it would be better this way,' he countered, lifting her chin, angling his head. 'For some say familiarity breeds contempt. Maybe we should consummate this marriage now, right now, lest in time you decide you hate me.'

His face drew closer and she remembered all the reasons why it shouldn't, remembered how she felt, remembered the promise that she'd made to herself. 'I already hate you.'

His nostrils flared, his eyes flared, then immediately descended into utter blackness. She knew she was playing with fire. 'In which case, sweet princess, what is the point of waiting? Let's finish this now.'

'No!' She pushed against his chest with every bit of strength she could muster, twisting away from him, almost stumbling in her hurry to get away. 'Get out! I do not want this! I do not want you!'

'You are fooling yourself, Princess,' he said, his chest heaving as his eyes burned like coals. 'Once again your body betrays you. Why shouldn't we finish what we started?'

'I'll tell you why,' she said. 'Because if you do not leave now, if you do not go, then it will be on your own head. And you need never seek my respect or love or even the tiniest shred of civility, because I will hate you as much as it is physically possible to hate anyone if you take what is not freely given!'

There were sparks spitting fire in her eyes, there was a bright slash of colour across her cheeks, and right now he burned for her—burned for this woman who was now his wife and yet not completely. He burned bright and hot, his blood heated and heavy in his groin, and it took every bit of the restraint civilisation had wrought over the aeons upon the male mind that he did not throw her bodily to the floor and take her now.

'Then I warn you, Princess. Do not take too long to decide to give what you must, because when it all comes down to it, for the sake of Al-Jirad, I will gladly risk your hatred!'

He left her then and his blood turned to steam, his fury a living thing, tangling in his gut, fuelling his feet into long, purposeful strides. He should never have given her time to prepare. He should have accompanied her to his suite, got their necessary coupling over and done with before returning to his studies. Instead he had got lost in the endless pages and had given her too much time, it seemed. Time to think and plan and plot how she could evade her duty.

But it would not last.

In three days he would be crowned King of Al-Jirad, and like it or not, the princess must by then be his wife in all senses of the word. He had studied the pact in detail long enough to know that, searching for any way out, for any concessions.

He headed back to the library, back to his endless books and study. There was no point wasting time thinking about a spoilt princess and her pathetic, 'I will not sleep with anyone I do not know' now.

She would know him soon enough.

Her resistance would not last.

He could not afford to let it.

He'd already churned his way through twenty laps when he noticed Bahir at the end of the pool, and he cursed his decision not to return to his studies.

'You're up early,' his friend said, sitting himself down on the edge of the pool as Zoltan finished the lap and checked his watch. 'Barely six a.m. Honeymoon already over?'

Zoltan glared at him as he made a rapid change of plans. The ten extra laps could wait. He put his hands on the side of the pool and powered himself out, intending to grab his towel and just keep right on walking. He wasn't in the mood to talk to anyone this morning, let alone one of these clowns. They knew far too much about him as it was.

'Uh oh,' Bahir said behind him. 'Maybe the honeymoon hasn't even begun.'

'I didn't say anything,' Zoltan protested as he bent down to scoop up his towel.

'Brother, you didn't need to. It's written all over your body language. What happened? How could the princess manage to turn down the legendary Zoltan charm? Although admittedly all that brooding intensity must be tiresome to endure.'

He glared at his so-called friend. 'There's nothing to tell.'

Bahir grinned. 'So long as it's not because she plays for the other team.' He whistled. 'That would be one cruel waste.'

The urge to laugh battled with the urge to growl. He didn't want anyone speculating about his wife's sexuality. Besides, if Bahir only knew which team she'd openly speculated they all played for he wouldn't think it nearly as funny himself. He sighed. Clearly Bahir would not stop until he knew. 'She says it's because she doesn't know me.'

'What?'

He shrugged. 'She says she won't sleep with any

man she doesn't know. Apparently—' he ground out the words between his teeth '—that includes her husband.'

'But she has to. I thought you said so.'

'I did. According to the terms of the pact she has no choice.'

'Did you tell her that?'

He thought back to their argument and how bitter and twisted it had become at the end. 'Under the circumstances, I really don't think it would have helped if I had.'

'But she has to eventually, right? She has to give you heirs and she knows that?'

'True.'

'So don't tell anyone in the meantime,' Bahir said, shrugging. 'I won't tell if you won't, kind of thing.'

He shook his head. 'That won't work. I have to swear on the book of Al-Jirad that we are married in every sense of the word. '

'So lie.'

He shook his head. 'That is hardly an honourable way to start my reign.' He'd spent hours last night trying to work a way around the requirement—had lingered some time over that very option—until finally concluding that lying would not work even if he could bring himself to act so dishonourably. Besides, she would know the truth and she could hold that over him the entire time. It would not work if she could bring down the kingdom at any moment she chose.

His friend nodded. 'True. Still, I can see her point of view.'

'What's that supposed to mean?'

'Well, it has all been kind of sudden.'

'It's been sudden for everyone. And it's not as if she has a choice.'

'So maybe that's what this is all about. She wants to feel like it is her choice.'

Zoltan looked up. 'What are you talking about? Why should that matter?'

'She's a woman.' He shrugged. 'They think differently. Especially Jemeyan princesses.'

Zoltan looked at him. 'So what did happen between you and her sister?'

It was Bahir's turn to look uncomfortable. 'It's history. It doesn't matter. What you have to worry about is how your princess feels right now. She's a princess in a desert kingdom who has probably been hanging out all these years for her prince to turn up. She wants to be romanced. Instead she gets lumbered with you and told she has to make babies.' He shrugged. 'Frankly, who could blame her? Nothing personal, but who wouldn't be a tad disappointed?'

'Thank you so much for that erudite summation of the situation.'

Bahir was back to his grinning best. 'My pleasure. So, what are you going to do?'

He snorted. 'I don't have time to do anything. I've got too much to do before the coronation as it is.'

'Well, you'd better do something, or by the sounds of it there won't be a coronation and Mustafa would be within his rights to come steal that pretty bride right out from under your nose—and next time he won't leave you a window open to rescue her.'

'I've been wondering about that,' Zoltan said. 'What was Mustafa waiting for? If he'd slept with her that would have been the end of it.'

'Maybe,' Bahir mused, 'he was waiting to be married?'

Zoltan shook his head. That didn't sound like the

Mustafa he knew. 'More likely he was so sure that no-body could find them that he thought there was no rush; he could take his time torturing her by telling her in exquisite detail exactly what he had planned for her.'

'Then it's lucky we found her in time.'

Was it? Zoltan wondered as he padded back into the palace. She sure as hell didn't think so. He was still thinking about the words Bahir had used.

'She wants to feel like it is her choice.'

'She wants to be romanced.'

How could he do that? What was the point of even trying? Here in the palace it was like being in a fish-bowl, full of maids and footmen and the ever-present Hamzah, uncannily always to hand when he was needed and plenty of times when he was not. How was he sup-posed to romance her and somehow study the neces-sary texts to complete the formalities he was required to before he could be crowned King?

It was impossible.

And then he remembered it—a holiday his family had taken when he was just a child, a shared holiday with his uncle, the then-King, and his family. In a spot not far from the Blue Palace, a jewel of a location on a promontory reaching a sandy finger out into the sap-phire-blue sea. They had slept in tents listening to the waves on the shore at night, woken to the early-morning calls of gulls, fished, swum and ridden horses along the long, sandy beach.

Maybe he could take her there, where she could un-wind and relax and forget about duty and obligation for a while and maybe, just maybe, tolerate him long enough that they could consummate this marriage.

He could only hope.

* * *

'Where are we going again?' Aisha asked as the four-wheel drive tore up the desert highway. Outside the car was golden sands and shimmering heat, while inside was smooth leather and air-conditioned luxury. And the scent of him beside her was mixing with the leather, evocative, damnably alluring and much too likeable—much too annoying. She was almost tempted to open her window and risk the heat if it meant she wouldn't have to endure it.

'A place called Belshazzah on the coast,' Zoltan said without shifting his gaze from the road. The tracks of her nails, thankfully, were fading on his cheek. He stared at the road ahead, dodging patches of sand where the dunes crept over the road on their inexorable travels. A man in control, she thought, looking at him behind the wheel. A man used to taking charge, she guessed, unable to let someone else drive for him, so that the necessary bodyguards were forced to squeeze into the supply vehicles that trailed behind them. He looked good, his dark hands on the wheel, the folded-back sleeves of his white shirt contrasting with his corded forearms and that damned scent everywhere...

'How far is it?'

'Not far from the Blue Palace. No more than two hours away.'

Aisha buzzed down her window a few inches and sniffed.

'Are you cold?' he said, immediately moving to adjust the temperature.

'Not really,' she said, gazing out behind her dark glasses at a horizon bubbling under the desert sun. *Not at all.* When he'd turned up at her door this morning and asked if she'd like to accompany him to the beach encampment, she'd remembered the things he'd said to her last night and how close he'd come to forcing himself upon her and she'd almost told him where he could shove his beach encampment.

But something had stopped her. Whether it was the look in his eyes, that this unexpected invitation was costing him something, or whether it was just because for the first time he was actually asking if she would accompany him rather than telling her and riding roughshod over her opinions and views as was his usual tactic—whatever it was—she'd said yes.

'And remind me again why we're going there?'

He shrugged. 'The palace is too big, filled with too many people, too many advisers. I thought you might appreciate somewhere a little quieter.' He turned to her then. 'So we could get to know each other a little more.'

Even from behind his sunglasses she could feel the sizzle his eyes sent her all the way down to her toes.

'You mean so you can finally get what you expected you would get last night?'

He didn't look at her, but she caught his smile behind the wheel. 'Do you really think I need go to so much trouble when the palace is full of dark corners and secret places? Not exactly the kind of places you want to hang around and hold a meaningful conversation, but perfectly adequate for other, more carnal pleasures.'

Her window hummed even lower. She did not want to hear about dark places and carnal pleasures. Not when it made her body buzz with an electricity that felt uncannily like anticipation.

Impossible.

'It's not going to happen, you know,' she said, as much for her benefit as his.

'What?'

'I'm not going to sleep with you.'

'So you said.'

'I hate you.'

'You said that too. You made that more than plain last night.'

'Good. So long as we understand each other.'

'Oh,' he said, taking his eyes off the road to throw her a lazy smile, 'we may not know each other, but I think we understand each other perfectly.'

Dissatisfied with the way that conversation had ended, she fell silent for a while, looking out at the desert dunes, disappearing into the distance in all directions. She shuddered when she remembered another desert camp. 'How do you know Mustafa's not out here somewhere, waiting for you to make a mistake so he can steal me away and take the crown before you? Aren't you worried about him?'

'Are you scared, Princess? Are you worried now you should have consummated this marriage last night when you had the chance?'

She crossed her arms over her chest and turned her gaze pointedly out the window again. 'Definitely not.'

'Then you are braver than I thought. But you have nothing to fear. My sources say he's moved out of Al-Jirad for now.'

'So he knows he's beaten and given up?'

'Possibly.'

'And he won't be at the coronation?'

His jaw clenched, his hands tightening on the wheel. 'He wouldn't dare show his face.'

She hoped he was right. If she never saw the ugly slug again, it would be too soon. She looked around, wondering at the words he had spoken, about the punch his words had held. She wondered why he was so certain, and she guessed it was not all to do with her kidnapping.

'What did he do to you?'

There was a pause before he spoke. 'Why do you ask that?'

'You clearly hate him very much. He must have done something to deserve it.'

He snorted in response to that. 'You could say that. I grew up with him. I got to see how his twisted mind works first-hand.'

'Tell me.'

'Are you sure you want to hear this, Princess?'

'Is it so bad?'

'It is not pretty. He is not a nice person.'

She swallowed. 'I'm a big girl. I can handle it, surely.'

He nodded. 'As you say.' He looked back at the road for a moment before he began. 'There was a blind man in the village where we grew up, a man called Saleem,' he started. 'He was old and frail and everyone in the village looked out for him, brought him meals or firewood. He had a dog, a mutt he'd found somewhere that was his eyes. We used to pass Saleem's house on our way to school where Saleem was usually sitting outside, greeting everyone who passed. Mustafa never said anything, he just baited the dog every chance he got, teasing it, sometimes kicking it. One day he went too far and it bit him. I was with him that day, and I swear it was nothing more than a scratch, but Mustafa swore he would get even. Even when the old man told him that it was his fault—that even though he was blind he was not stupid. He knew Mustafa had been taunting his dog mercilessly all along.

'One day not long after, the dog went missing. The

whole village looked for it. Until someone found it—or, rather, what was left of it.'

She held her breath. 'What happened to it?'

'The dog had been tortured to within an inch of its life before something more horrible happened—something that said the killer had a grudge against not only the dog, but against its owner.'

'What do you mean?'

'The dog had been blinded. So, even if it had somehow managed to survive the torture, it would have been useless to Saleem.'

She shuddered, feeling sick. 'How could anyone do such a thing to an animal, a valued pet?'

'That one could.'

'You believe it was Mustafa?'

'I know it was him. I overheard him boasting to a schoolfriend in graphic detail about what he had done. He had always been a bully. He was proud of what he had done to a helpless animal.'

'Did you tell anyone?'

Her question brought the full pain and the injustice of the past crashing back. He remembered the fury of his father when he had told him what he had heard; fury directed not at Mustafa but at him for daring to speak ill of his favoured child. He remembered the savage beating he had endured for daring to speak the truth.

'I told someone. For all the good it did me.'

Choose your battles.

His uncle had been so right. There had been no point picking that one. He had never been going to win where Mustafa was concerned. Not back then.

She waited for more but he went quiet then, staring fixedly at the road ahead, so she turned to look out her own window, staring at the passing dunes, wondering what kind of person did something like that for kicks and wondering about all the things Zoltan wasn't telling her.

He was an enigma, this man she was married to, and, as much as she hated him for who and what he was and what he had forced her into, maybe she should be grateful she had been saved the alternative. Because she would have been Mustafa's wife if this man had not come for her. She shuddered.

'Princess?'

She looked around, blinking. 'Yes?'

'Are you all right? You missed my question.'

'Oh.' She sat up straight and lifted the heavy weight of the ponytail behind her head to cool her neck. 'I'm sorry. What did you ask?'

He looked at her for a moment, as if he wasn't sure whether to believe her or not, before looking back at the interminably long, straight road ahead. 'Seeing as we were talking about Mustafa,' he started.

'Yes?'

'There is something I don't understand. Something you told me when we rescued you.'

'Some rescue,' she said, but her words sounded increasingly hollow in the wake of Zoltan's revelations about his half-brother's cruel nature. Maybe he had saved her from a fate worse than death after all. 'What about it?' she said before she could explore that revelation any further.

'How did you convince Mustafa not to take you right then and there, while he had you in the camp? Why was he prepared to wait until the wedding? Because if Mustafa had laid claim to you that first night he held you captive, if he had had witnesses to the act, then no rescue could have prevented you from being his queen and him the new king.'

She swallowed back on a surge of memory-fed bile, not wanting to think back to those poisoned hours. 'He told me he did not care to wait, you are right.'

'So why did he? That does not sound like the Mustafa I know.'

She blinked against the sun now dipping low enough to intrude through her window and sat up straighter to avoid it, even if that meant she had to lean closer to him in the process, and closer to that damned evocative scent.

'Simple, really. I told him that he would be cursed if he took me before our wedding night.'

'You told him that and he believed you?'

'Apparently so.'

'But there must have been more reason than that. Why would he believe that he would be cursed?'

Beside him she swallowed. She didn't want to have to admit to him the truth, although she rationalised he would find that truth out some time. And maybe he might at least understand her reluctance to jump into bed and spread her legs for him as if the act itself meant nothing.

'Because I told him that, according to the Jemeyan tenets, if he took me before our wedding night the gods would curse him with a soft and shrivelled penis for evermore.'

'Because you are a princess?'

'Because I am a virgin.'

'And he believed you?' He laughed then as if it was the biggest joke in the world, and she wasn't tempted in the least to rake her nails down his laughing face again—this time she wanted to strangle him.

Instead she turned away, pretending to stare out of the window and at the sea, fat tears squeezing from her eyes, but only half from the humiliating memories of being poked and parted and prodded by the wiry fingers of some old crone who smelt like camel dung.

The other half was because it never occurred to Zoltan to believe her. It never occurred to him that she might be telling the truth, that she might actually be a virgin. And the rank injustice of it all was almost too much to bear. She angled her body away from him to mask the dampness that suddenly welled in her eyes.

To think she had saved herself all this time only to be bound to someone like him instead. The one thing she had always thought hers to give; the one thing she had thought hers to control, and when all was said and done she had no control at all. No choice. It was not to be given as a gift, but a due.

What a waste.

'It would seem your half-brother is superstitious,' she managed to say through her wretchedness to cover the truth.

And from behind the wheel, Zoltan's words sounded as though he was still smiling. 'Yes. He always was a fool.'

CHAPTER EIGHT

SHE could smell the salt on the air long before she could see the sea. They had left the highway some time ago. The track across the desert sands was slower going, until they topped one last dune and suddenly a dry desert world turned into paradise.

From their vantage point, she could see the rocky peninsula jutting into the crystal-clear sapphire waters, and where before she had seen no signs of vegetation beyond small, scrubby salt-bushes clinging to the sand for their meagre existence for miles, now the shores and rocks were dotted with palms, the rocky outcrops covered with lush, green vegetation.

'It's beautiful,' she said as they descended, heading for the long, white strip of sandy beach. 'But how?'

'A natural spring feeds this area. If you like, I will take you and show you where the water runs clean and pure from the earth. If I try hard enough, I'm sure I'll remember the way.'

The offer was so surprising, not only because he was asking her again, but because he had revealed a part of himself with his words—that he had been here before, and clearly a long time ago.

'I would like that,' she said, wondering what he would have been like as a child. Overbearing, like he was now? Although that wasn't strictly true, she was forced to admit. He wasn't overbearing *all* the time.

Which was a shame, really, because he was much easier to hate when he was. And she didn't want to find reason not to hate him, because then she might be tempted to wonder…

But no. She shook her head, shaking out the thought. She didn't wonder. She didn't care. She didn't want to know what it would be like to be made love to by a man like this one, who clearly was no virgin himself, who had no doubt had many lovers and who probably knew all about women and what they might enjoy…

'Is something wrong, Princess?'

She looked up at him, startled. 'No. Why do you ask?'

'Because you made some kind of sound, kind of like a whimper. I wondered if there was something wrong.'

'No.' She turned away, her cheeks burning up. 'I'm fine, just sick of sitting down. Are we nearly there?'

Thankfully they were. A cluster of tents had been erected below a stand of palm trees in preparation for their arrival, one set apart from the rest.

'Is that one mine?' she asked, half-suspecting, half-dreading the answer.

'That one is ours, Princess,' he said, pulling open her door and offering her his hand to climb from the car. 'It would not do to let everyone know the true state of our marriage.'

'But I told you…'

He found it hard not to grind his teeth together. So she had—how many times already? Did she think he wanted to be reminded how much she did not want to lie with him? 'I am sure you will be more than satisfied with the sleeping arrangements.'

She looked down at his hand, as if assessing whether he was telling the truth. 'Fine,' she said, finally accepting his offer of assistance. 'But, if not, then I will not be held accountable for the bruise on your ego.'

'I'm sure my ego can take it, Princess. It is the damage you do to the monarchy that is my more immediate concern, and indeed the damage you could do to your own father's. So perhaps you might keep that in mind.'

Her face closed, as if she'd pulled all the shutters down to retreat into herself.

So be it.

She might be used to having things all her way when she was at home leading her sheltered spoilt-princess life, but she was here now, she was his wife, and she would start doing her duty and acting like his wife before they left and before the coronation. Nothing was surer.

Still, for what it was worth, he let her lead the way into their tent to inspect the sleeping arrangements, to check out the large sofa that could double for a bed if needed, and the large bed he was hoping would be the only sleeping arrangement required.

Besides, following her was hardly a hardship. Not when he had the chance to check out the rhythmic sway of her hips under the coral-coloured abaya she wore today.

As he followed her he could not work out whether he liked her dressed more like this—in a cool cotton robe that only hinted at the shape beneath, but did so seductively and unexpectedly when a helpful on-shore breeze ventured along and pushed the fabric against her shape— or in trousers, like she'd worn that first day at the palace, that fitted her shape and accentuated her curves.

Then again, he hadn't yet seen her without her clothes. And, while he'd felt the firmness of her flesh under his hands, and felt the delicious curve of her belly and roundness of her bottom hard against him, there was still that delicious pleasure to come.

Now, there was something to think about…

She turned, her hand on the tent flap, just about to enter. 'Did you say something?'

'No,' he said, struggling to adjust to the conscious world. 'Why do you ask?'

'Because I thought you said something. Though, now I think of it, it sounded more like a groan. Are you sure you're all right?'

But before he could find the words to answer, she had angled her head to the notes being carried intermittently on the breeze. 'What's that?'

Never had he been more grateful for a change of topic as he strained his ears to listen. The knowledge that she had made him so oblivious to his own reactions was a cold wake-up call. He could not afford to let such lapses happen, not if he was to be King.

And suddenly the notes made sense on the breeze and reminded him of something he'd been told. 'There is a camp of wandering tribes people nearby. A few families, nothing more. They will shortly move on, as they do.'

'They are safe, then, these tribes people?'

And he realised that even to ask that question showed she wasn't as unconcerned at the thought of being re-captured by Mustafa as she wanted him to think.

'They would not be here if they were not. But they have been advised of our coming and they value their privacy too. So rest assured, Princess, they will keep their distance and they will not harm you.'

* * *

She'd only been here an hour and already she loved it. Being on the coast meant on-shore breezes that took the sting from the heat of the day and made being on sand a pleasure, rather than torture—at least if you had taken off your sandals to paddle your feet in the shallows.

And she hadn't minded a bit when Zoltan had had to excuse himself to take care of 'business', whatever that meant. Because it gave her the chance to truly relax. Despite all the beauty of this place, the endless sapphire waters, the calming sway of palm trees and the eternal, soothing whoosh of tide, there was no relaxing with that man about.

But still, she was glad she had come. Already, without the overwhelming weight of the palace and the duty it carried, she felt lighter of spirit. She knew there was no way of evading that duty for long. She knew she could not forever evade the chore that life had thrown her way.

But for now the long beach had beckoned her, drawing her to the point at the end of the peninsula, and she was thinking it was time to return when she heard it, the cry of a child in distress.

It came on the breeze, and disappeared just as quickly, and for a moment she thought she'd imagined it or misread the cry of a sea bird, and already she'd turned for the walk back when she heard it again. Her feet stilled in the shallows. A child was definitely crying nearby and there was no hint of any soothing reply to tell her anyone had heard or was taking any notice.

She swivelled in the shallows, picked up the hem of her abaya in one hand and ran down the beach towards the headland as fast as she could.

It was only when she rounded the rocky outcrop at the end she found the child sitting in the sand and wailing. She looked around and saw no-one, only this young girl squealing and clutching at her foot. Her bleeding foot.

'Hello,' she said tentatively as the girl looked up at her with dark, suspicious eyes, her sobs momentarily stopping on a hiccup. 'What's wrong?'

The young girl sniffed and looked down at her foot, saw the blood and wailed again.

Aisha kneeled down beside her. 'Let me look,' she said. She took her foot gently in her hands and saw a gash seeping blood, a broken shell nearby, dagger sharp, that she must have trod on with her bare feet.

'Ow! It hurts!' the young girl cried, and Aisha put a hand behind her head, stroking her hair to soothe her.

'I'm sorry, but I'm going to have to wrap this up and it might hurt a little bit.' She looked around, wishing for someone—anyone—to appear. Surely someone must realise their child was missing and take charge so she didn't have to? Because she had nothing with her that might help, and the swaying palm trees offered no assistance, no rescue.

'Where is your mother?' she asked, once again scanning the palms for any hint of the girl's family as she ripped the hem of her abaya, tearing a long strip from the bottom and yanking it off at the seam. She folded the fabric until it formed a bandage she could wrap around the child's foot.

'Katif was crying. And Mama ran back to the camp and told me to follow.' And then she shrieked and Aisha felt guilty for tying the bandage so tight, even when she knew the girl was upset about not being able to follow her mother and her mother not coming back.

'Your mother knows you are okay,' she soothed, sensing it was what the child needed to hear. 'Your mother is busy with Katif right now, but she knew I would look out for you and she could check on you later.'

The girl blinked up at her. 'You know my mother?'

There was no way she could lie. 'No, but I know she is good to be taking care of Katif, and I know someone will be here soon for you.'

And even as she spoke there was a panicked cry as a woman emerged running from the trees. 'Cala! Cala!'

'Mama!'

'Oh, Cala,' she said, relief evident in her voice as she fell to the sand and squeezed her child tightly in her arms. 'I am so sorry, I did not see you fall behind.' And then she noticed the improvised bandage on her daughter's foot. 'But what happened?'

'I cut my foot on a shell. This lady found me.'

For the first time the woman took notice of Aisha. 'The wound will need cleaning before it can be properly dressed,' Aisha offered. 'There was not much I could do here.'

The mother nodded, her tear-streaked face caked with sand. 'Thank you for taking care of her. Katif was screaming again; he's sick and I don't know what's wrong with him but I had to get him back to camp and I thought Cala was right behind me.' She gulped in air as she rocked her child in her arms. 'I was so afraid when I realised she was missing. I was so worried.'

Aisha stroked her arm. 'It's all right. Cala is fine.' She looked over her shoulder, thinking that she should be getting back. 'I must go. Will you be all right getting back to camp?'

'Of course,' the mother said, letting go of her child for a moment to take Aisha's hand and press her forehead to it, noticing the torn hem of her robe. 'Oh, but you have ruined your abaya.'

'It is nothing, really. I have many more.'

And the woman really looked at her this time, her eyes widening in shock, tears once again welling from their dark depths. 'Blessings to you,' she said, prostrating herself on the sand before her as her wide-eyed daughter looked on, contentedly sucking on two fingers of her hand. 'Bless you.'

'What are you doing?' she asked Zoltan when she returned. All the way back she had felt the sun warm her skin. All the way back she had felt the warmth of the woman's blessings in her heart.

Now she found Zoltan sitting at a desk under the shade of a palm tree, a massive tome before him.

He barely looked up from his study. 'It was too hot inside the tent.'

'No, I mean, what are you reading?'

He looked up then, suddenly scowling when he saw her torn robe. 'What happened to your abaya?'

She looked down. 'Oh, there was a child on the beach. She'd cut her foot.'

He leaned back in his chair, his frown deepening. 'And so you tore your robe?'

She shrugged. 'There was nothing else to use.' And then she remembered. 'Is there a doctor somewhere close?'

This time he stood. 'Are you hurt, Princess?'

'No, not for me. There is a child—a baby, I think. It sounds like he should be seen by a doctor. The mother is worried...' He was looking at her strangely. 'What's wrong?'

He shook his head. 'Nothing. And yes, Ahab—one of the chefs—has some medical expertise. I will ask him to visit the camp, to see if there is anything he can do.'

She nodded, majorly relieved. 'Thank you. It is probably worth him checking the cut on the girl's foot too, in case there is still some shell lodged inside.' She looked down at her torn robe. 'I should get changed.'

He watched her turn, wondering about a spoilt princess who would tear her own abaya to make a bandage for a child she didn't know. A stranger.

And he didn't want her to go. He slammed the book shut. He'd had enough of crusty old prose for one day. Besides, he was supposed to be getting to know her.

'Princess, seeing you're getting changed...?'

'Yes?'

'Now that the sun is past its worst, I was thinking of taking a swim to cool down. Would you care to join me?'

He saw a slideshow of emotions flash over her eyes: uncertainty, fear, even a glimmer of panic, but then she gave a longing look out at the ocean, where the water sparkled and beckoned and promised cool, clear relief under the dipping sun.

He recognised the moment she decided before she'd said the words, in the decisive little pout of her lips.

'Yes,' she said, with a nod. 'Why not?'

It's only a swim, she told herself as Zoltan went to instruct Ahab and she changed into her swimsuit. *In bright daylight and in clear sight of the beach.*

It wasn't as though he could actually try anything.

But that didn't stop her skin from tingling as she pulled on her tangerine-coloured one-piece, didn't stop the tiny hairs on the back of her neck from lifting or stop her remembering how good he had looked wearing nothing but a black band of lycra.

Only a swim.

She belted a robe around herself and tugged it tight

before pinning her hair up. If she got into the water before he returned to get changed himself, it wasn't as though he would even see her.

The beach was deserted. She dropped her towel and sunglasses on one of the recliners that had been put there expressly for their use, and, with a final look over her shoulder to check that Zoltan was nowhere to be seen, she slipped off her robe and padded to the sea.

It was warm in the shallows, so no shock to the system, the temperature dropping as the water deepened, cool currents swirling around her knees and sliding inexorably higher with each incoming wave. She waded deeper into the crystal-clear sea, her hands trailing through the water by her sides until her thighs tingled with the delicious contrast of cool and heat and she dived under an incoming wave to truncate the exquisite torture.

She was a goddess. There was no other way to describe her that could possibly do her justice. And he thanked whatever gods were watching over him that had brought him to this part of the beach at this particular moment in time. He'd witnessed her furtive glance over her shoulder and watched her wade into the sea, all long, honey-gold limbs and sweeping curves, the sweetly seductive roll of her hips like a siren's call.

He growled low in his throat.

He had never been one to resist the call of a siren. Even one who at the same time appeared so timid and shy. Why was she so nervous around him? Because she knew what was in store for her?

No. Because she knew what she did to him and she wished it wasn't so.

Because she felt it herself.

He watched her strike out in the water, swimming expertly along the shore, long, effortless-looking strokes, measured and effective, the kick of her feet propelling her along.

Dressed in that colour she looked like a luscious piece of fruit.

A piece of fruit he could not wait to sample.

And as his groin ached and tightened he thought that maybe this swim wasn't going to provide quite the cooling-off he'd had in mind.

The water was delicious, the repetitive rhythm of her strokes soothing in its own way, and a swim was turning out to be a very good idea. Until something grabbed hold of her ankle and pulled tight.

She screamed and tugged and whatever it was let go. She came up spluttering, coughing sea water, and pushed a tangle of hair out of her eyes.

'You!' she said between coughs when she found Zoltan standing there grinning at her. 'It's not funny. You scared the hell out of me.'

'Did you think you'd caught a shark, Princess?'

'A shark would be preferable,' she spat back and dived under the water to swim away. He was alongside her when she came up for air. 'It's a big ocean, you know. Go find your own bit to play in.'

'Your strap is twisted,' he said, ignoring her frustration and building on it by putting a hand to her shoulder, slipping his fingers underneath the strap and gently turning it up the right way. She gasped as his fingers brushed her skin, turning it to goose bumps and her nipples to hard peaks as he left his hand there longer than he needed. 'That colour suits you, Princess. You look good enough to eat.'

Nothing could stop the heat from flooding her face or the heavy, aching need pooling between her thighs. He was so big before her, so powerful, his shoulders broad, his chest dripping wet, and it was all she could do not to reach out a hand and feel if his skin felt as good as it looked.

She yanked her eyes away, looked to the shore. 'I should go back.'

'Already?'

'I had a head start. And I need to wash my hair.'

He smiled one of those wide, lazy smiles that made his face look boyish, even a little bit handsome. 'So you did. But of course you must go, Princess. Such a pressing need must be urgently addressed.'

She knew he was laughing at her but she almost didn't mind. Worse still, she almost found herself wishing he would make her stay. *Which made no sense at all.*

CHAPTER NINE

HER hair was almost dry when he found her brushing it in a chair under the palms. The air was filled with the scent of lamb on the spit and at first she assumed it must be time to eat.

'You have a visitor, Princess,' he said. 'Or several of them, to be more precise.'

'Me?' She put her brush down and followed him.

They stood in a small group, looking uncertain and talking quietly amongst themselves—a woman holding a baby, a man alongside and a little girl holding a small package in her hands.

The girl from the beach.

When the woman saw her she broke into a wide smile, tears once again welling in her eyes, but it was the man who stepped forward. 'I am so sorry,' he said with a bow. 'I told Marisha this was a bad time, but she insisted we come and thank you both. But you see, the helicopter comes soon after dawn tomorrow morning.'

She looked across at Zoltan to see if he understood and the mother came forward. 'Princess, Katif needs a small operation—his coughing has torn his muscles and they need to stitch it up so he will not cry any more. They are coming to take us to the hospital and I will not have a chance to thank you again.'

She reached down and urged the young girl forward with a pat to her head. 'Now, Cala.'

The little girl blinked up at her, and suddenly seemed to remember the package. She stepped tentatively forward, limping a little on her tender foot, a bandage strapped around it under her satin slipper. 'This is for you.'

Aisha smiled down at her. 'You didn't have to bring me a present.'

'We wanted to, Princess,' the mother said. 'To replace the abaya you ruined to bandage Cala's foot.'

Aisha knelt down and touched a hand to Cala's head. 'How is your foot now, Cala? Is it still hurting?'

'It hurts, but the doctor-man fixed it.'

And she smiled her thanks up at Zoltan, who was watching her, a strange expression on his face.

'It will feel better soon, I promise,' she said, accepting the parcel and pulling the end of the bow till the ribbon fluttered open. She pulled back the wrapping and gasped.

'It is all hand-stitched, Princess,' the woman offered proudly as Aisha lifted the delicate garment spun from golden thread and gossamer-thin.

'It's beautiful,' she said, fingering the detailed embroidery around the neckline. 'It must have taken months.'

The woman beamed with pride. 'My family has always been known for our needlework. It was the least your generosity deserved.'

Aisha gathered the little girl in her arms and hugged her. 'Thank you, Cala.' Then she rose and hugged her mother too, careful of the now-sleeping baby in her arms. 'Thank you. I shall wear it with honour and remember you always.'

She looked across at Zoltan and wondered if she should ask him first, but then decided it didn't matter.

'You will stay and eat with us, won't you?'

The adults looked unsure, clearly not expecting the invitation, not knowing if she was serious. 'We did not mean to intrude.'

'You are not intruding,' she assured them, hoping Zoltan thought the same.

'Please, Mama,' Cala said, tugging on her mother's robe. 'Please can we stay?'

'Of course,' Zoltan said in that commanding voice he had, as if there was never any question. 'You must stay.'

They sat on cushions around a campfire, supping on spiced lamb with yoghurt and mint, with rice and okra, washing it down with honeyed tea under a blanket of stars. Afterwards, with the fragrant scent of the sisha pipe drifting from the cook's camp, Cala's father produced his ney reed pipe from somewhere in his robes and played more of that haunting music she had heard wafting over the headland when they had first arrived.

Cala edged closer and closer to the princess as the music wove magic in the night sky until she wormed her way under her arm and onto her lap. 'Cala,' her mother berated.

'She's fine,' Aisha assured her.

The girl looked up at her with big, dark eyes. 'Are you really a princess?'

Aisha smiled. 'Yes, it's true.'

'Where's your crown?'

She laughed. 'I don't wear a crown every day.'

'Oh.' The girl sounded disappointed. 'Is Princess your name?'

'No. Princess is my job, like calling someone "doctor" or "professor". Of course I have a real name. My name is Aisha.'

Aisha.

Moon goddess.

Strange. He had never thought about her having a name. He had always thought of her simply as 'princess', but how appropriate she would have a name like that. Little wonder she looked like a goddess.

And here she was, his precious little spoilt princess, cuddling a child and looking every bit as much a mother as the child's own mother did.

This woman would bear his children.

She would sit like that in a few years from now and it would be his children clambering over her. It would be the product of his seed she would cuddle and nurture.

And the vision was so powerful, so compelling, that something indescribable swelled inside him and he wished for it to be true.

Aisha. Sitting there with near-strangers, giving of herself to people who possessed little more than the clothes on their back and who had gifted her probably their most treasured possession. Giving herself to *his* people.

Maybe she was not such a spoilt princess after all.

And the thought was so foreign when it came that he almost rejected it out of hand. Almost. But the proof was right there in front of him. Maybe there was more to her after all.

'Thank you,' she said after the family had gone and they walked companionably along the shoreline under a sliver of crescent moon. It had seemed the most obvious thing in the world to do. The night was balmy and inviting, and he knew that she was not yet ready to fall into his bed, but he was in no hurry to return to his study of the centuries-old texts.

'What are you thanking me for?'

'Lots of things,' she said. 'For sending Ahab to look at their children, for one. For arranging the necessary transport to hospital for the operation Katif needs, if not the operation itself. And for not minding that the family shared our meal.'

'Be careful, Princess,' he warned, holding up one hand. 'Or one might almost forget that you hate me.'

She blinked, though whether she was trying to gauge how serious he was, or whether she had been struck with the same revelation, he could not be sure. 'So you have some redeeming features. I wouldn't go reading too much into it.' But he noticed her words lacked the conviction and fire of her earlier diatribes. He especially noticed that she didn't insist that she did hate him. He liked that she didn't feel the compunction to tell him. He sighed into the night breeze. It had been right to get out of the palace where everything was so formal and rigid, where every move was governed by protocol.

In the palace there was always someone watching, even if it was only someone on hand and waiting to find out if there was anything one needed. For all its space, in the palace it was impossible to move without being seen. He curled his fingers around hers as they walked: in the palace it would have been impossible to do *this* without his three friends betting amongst themselves whether it meant that he would score tonight.

'You were good with that child,' he said, noticing— *liking*—that she didn't pull her hand away. 'I suspect you found a fan.'

'Cala is very likeable.'

'You were equally good with her family, making

them feel special. If you can be like that with everyone, you will make a great sheikha. You will be a queen who will be well-loved.'

She stopped and pulled her hand free, rubbing her hands on her arms so he could not reclaim it. 'If I'd imagined this walk was going to provide you with yet another opportunity to remind me of the nature of this marriage, and of my upcoming *duty* in your bed, I never would have agreed to come along.'

He cursed his clumsy efforts to praise her. 'I am sorry, Princess. I did not mean...'

She blinked up at him, her aggravation temporarily overwhelmed by surprise. He was sorry? He was actually sorry and he was telling her so? Was this Zoltan the barbarian sheikh before her?

But then, he wasn't all barbarian, she had to concede. Otherwise why would he have sent anyone to look at a sick child? Why would he have approved his uplift in a helicopter, no less, and the required operation if he was a monster?

'No, I'm sorry,' she said, holding up her hands as she shook her head. 'There was no need for me to respond that way. I overreacted.' *Because I'm the one who can't stop thinking about doing my duty...*

The night was softly romantic, it was late, soon it would be time for bed and she was here on this beach with a man who came charged with electricity.

'What did you do before?' she asked, changing the subject before he too realised why she was so jumpy, resuming her walk along the beach under the stars. 'Before all this happened. Were you always in Al-Jirad? I attended a few functions at the Blue Palace, but I don't remember seeing you at any of them.'

'No, you wouldn't have,' he said, falling into step

beside her as the low waves swooshed in, their foam
bright even in the low moonlight. 'I left when it was
clear there was no place for me here.'

'Because of Mustafa?'

'Partly. My father always took his side. I was twelve
when my mother died and there seemed no reason to
stay. Mustafa and I hated each other and everyone knew
it. For the peace of the family, my father sent me to
boarding school in England.'

She looked up at his troubled profile and wondered
what it must have been like to be cast adrift from your
family because you didn't fit in, when you were possibly the only sane member in it.

She slipped her hand back in his and resumed walking along the shore, hoping he wouldn't make too much
of it. She was merely offering her understanding, that
was all. 'Is that where you met your three friends?'

'That was later. We met at university.'

'And you clicked right away?'

'No. We hated each other on sight.'

She looked at him and frowned. He shrugged.
'Nothing breeds hatred faster than someone else telling you who should be friends.'

'I don't think I understand.'

'It's a long story. Basically we'd all come from different places and somehow all ended up in the university
rowing club, all of us loners up till then and intending
to row alone, as we had always done to keep fit. Until
someone decided to stick us in a crew together, expecting we "foreigners" should all get along. For a joke they
called our four the *Sheikh Caique*.' He paused a while,
reflecting, and then said, 'They did not laugh long.'

'And over time you did become good friends with
them.'

He shrugged and looked out to sea, and she wondered what parts of the story he was not telling her. 'That was not automatic, but yes. And I could not wish for better brothers.'

They walked in silence for a while, the whoosh of the waves and the call of birds settling down to sleep in the swaying palm trees the music of the night.

And then he surprised her by stopping and catching her other hand in his. 'I owe you an apology,' he started.

'No, I explained—'

He let go of one hand and put a finger to her lips. 'I need to say this, Princess, and I am not good at apologies, so you must not stop me.'

She nodded, her lips brushing the pad of his finger, and she drank in the intoxicating scent of him. It was all she could do not to reach out her tongue so she might once again taste his flesh.

'I was wrong about you, Princess. I know I messed up trying to tell you before, but you are not who I thought you were. I underestimated you. I assumed you were lightweight and frothy, spoilt and two-dimensional. I assumed that because you called what you did with children your "work", that it must be no kind of work. But after seeing you forge a bond with that little girl today, the way you knelt down and listened to her and treated her like an equal, I realised this is a gift you have.

'And I apologise unreservedly for my misjudgement, because I was wrong on every single count. I had no concept of the person you really are.'

She waited for reality to return—for this moment to pass, this dream sequence to pass, for the real Zoltan to return—but instead she saw only this Zoltan waiting for her answer.

'You're wrong, you know.'

'About you?'

'About being no good at apologies. That was one of the best I think I've ever heard.'

It was true. His confession had reached out to her, warming her in places she would never have suspected him reaching. His previous assessment of her was no surprise. She had known he had resented her from the start, assuming she was some shallow party-girl princess who cared nothing for duty. But what was a surprise was the way his words touched her. And, even though he had not realised yet in how many ways he had misjudged her, his words touched her in places deep inside, places she thought immune to the likes of anything Zoltan could say or do.

He smiled. 'I am so sorry, Aisha,' he said and she blinked up open-mouthed at him.

'You called me by my name. You have never called me that before.'

He nodded, his eyes contrite. 'And it is to my eternal shame that I did not do so from the very beginning. You deserved to be called by your name rather than your title. A name that spoke of the goddess you were surely named for, the goddess who must be so jealous right now of your perfection that she is hiding away up there behind the blinds.'

And, even though he'd gone too far, she could not help but smile. 'You should not suggest such things of the gods,' she said, still battling to find balance in a world suddenly shifted off its axis. 'Lest they grow jealous and seek their revenge against the mortal.'

'A goddess could be jealous of you,' he said, curling his hand around her neck. 'Except that you are bound in marriage to me, and no goddess could possibly ever envy you that. They would figure you are already paying the price for your beauty.'

She swallowed, wondering where the other Zoltan was hiding, the one who would come out at any moment breathing hell-fire and damnation and demanding that she do her duty by him, if not willingly, at least for the good of their respective countries.

Yet she didn't want that other Zoltan to appear, because this Zoltan made her feel so good—not only because he awakened all her senses, but because he spoke to her needs and desires and touched her in dark, secret places she had never known existed.

'Do you have an evil twin?' she asked on impulse, remembering another conversation where he had implied the same of her, because she needed something—anything—to lighten the tone of this conversation and defuse the intensity she felt building inside.

His lips turned up. 'Not that I know of.'

She smiled as she shook her head and looked up into his dark eyes, wondering if it would be some kind of sin if she wanted to enjoy this other Zoltan just a little while longer. 'I'm not entirely convinced.' She allowed her smile to widen. 'Because this twin I wouldn't mind getting to know a little better. If I thought he was going to stick around a while, that is.'

He dragged in a breath, his dark eyes looking perplexed, even a little tortured. 'I'm not sure that's possible,' he said, his gaze fixed on her mouth. 'Because right now I want to kiss you. And I'm not sure I should. I'm not sure which twin you might end up with.'

'Maybe,' she said a little breathlessly, watching his mouth draw nearer, 'there's only one way to find out. Maybe we just have to risk it.'

Something flared and caught fire in his eyes. 'I think you might be right.'

He dipped his head, curled one hand around her neck and drew her slowly closer, pausing mere millimetres away, forcing their breath to curl and mingle between them, a prelude to the dance to come.

Then even that scant separation was gone as he pressed his lips to hers.

One touch of her lips and he remembered—sweet and spice; honey, cinnamon and chili; sweet and spice with heat. But there was so much more besides.

For this night she tasted of moonlight and promises, of soft desert nights and whispered secrets. She tasted of woman.

All woman.

He groaned against her mouth, let his arms surround her, drawing her into his embrace. She came willingly, accepting his invitation, until her breasts were hard up against his chest, her slim body curving into his, supple and lithe, while he supped of her lush mouth. And when he felt her hands on his back, felt her nails raking his skin through his shirt, he wanted to lift his head and roar with victory, for the goddess would be his tonight.

Except there was no way he was leaving this kiss.

She was drowning. One touch of his lips and the air had evaporated in her lungs and it was sensation that now swamped her, sensation that rolled over her, wave after delicious wave. His lips on hers, his taste in her mouth, his arms around her and her body knowing just one thing.

Need.

It bloomed under the surprisingly gentle caress of his lips. It took root and spread a tangle of branches to every other place he touched. It built on itself, growing, becoming more powerful and insistent.

He held her face in his hands and kissed her eyes, her nose, her chin before returning to her waiting lips, seducing her with his hot mouth while her hands drank in his tight flesh.

And in the midst of it all she wondered, how could this be the same man who had kissed her in the library? The same man who had so cruelly punished her with his kiss and had demanded her presence in his suite so he could impregnate her with his seed?

Yet it must be the same man, for she recognised him by his taste and his essence and the far-reaching impact he had upon her body.

But in between the layers of passion and the on-slaught of sensation, in between the breathless plea-sure, a niggling kernel of doubt crept in: how could he be so different now and yet still be the same person?

'Aisha,' he said, breathing as heavily as she, resting his forehead on hers, his nose against hers. She almost forgot to care that he seemed different, because he was so warm now, so wonderful, and the way he said her name made her tremble with desire. This man, who was now her husband. That thought made her shudder anew.

'You are a goddess,' he said, his big hand scooping over her shoulder and down, inexorably down, to cup one achingly heavy breast. Breath jagged in her throat, her senses momentarily shorting before he brushed the pad of his thumb against her nipple and she gasped as her entire circuitry lit up with exquisite pleasure that made her inner thighs hum.

She mewled with pleasure. 'I think,' she uttered, breathless with desire, 'maybe you must be the evil twin after all.'

And he growled out a laugh that worked its way into her bones and stroked her from the inside out. 'Make love to me, Aisha,' he said, before his lips found hers again. 'Be my goddess tonight.'

Tonight?

Already?

But before she could protest and say it was too soon, he sucked her back into his kiss with his hot mouth and his dangerous tongue and drew her close against him, shocking her when she felt his rigid heat hard against her, frightening her with the realisation that she must take that part of him inside her body. And, even though her logical mind told her that men and women the world over made love this way and had done for centuries, the unknown was equally as persuasive. Surely not all men were so large? How was she—the untested—supposed to accommodate him? There was no way he could not know she was a virgin. There was no way it would not hurt.

Yet something about that rigid column pressing against her belly, something wild and wanton that was written on the pulsing insistence of her own body, made her yearn to try.

'Please,' she cried between frantic breaths, not knowing let alone understanding what she was asking for as he dipped his head to her breast and suckled her nipple in his hot, hot mouth, sending spears of sensation shooting down to where her blood pulsed loud and urgent between her thighs.

'Aisha,' he said, his breathing as wild as hers as he reclaimed her mouth, her lips already tender from the rub of his whiskered cheeks. She wondered why she was hesitating and not already in his bed.

It wasn't as if she had a choice. She was already married to this man. She was expected to bear his children and provide the country with heirs, and the officials would already be counting the days.

Why should she wait when the night was so perfect and her own need so insistent?

Why wait, when she already hungered to discover more?

His mouth wove magic on her throat, his hands turned her flesh molten and made her shudder with delight, and through it all she sensed the greater pleasures that were yet to be discovered, yet to come.

And still a crack opened in the midst of her longing, a flaw in the building intensity of feeling, a space in which to give rein to her doubts and fears.

For this was not how she had planned her first time to be.

Even though her breasts were heavy with want, and her body pressed itself closer to this man of its own wicked accord, this was not how she had imagined giving away her most private, guarded possession.

She had wanted to give it up with love, not merely in the heated flames of lust.

She had wanted to give it to a man she loved because she wanted to. Because she had made that choice.

And through that widening crack came the mantra, the words she'd rehearsed and practised and that had seemed so important to cling to.

'I won't sleep with you,' she breathed. Yet she faltered over the words even as she spoke them out loud, struggling to comprehend what they meant and why they had suddenly seemed so very necessary to say, why they now seemed so strangely hollow.

'But that is good news,' he said, his mouth at her throat, his hands scooping down the curve of her back to press her even closer to him, 'because I don't want you asleep. When I make love to you, I want you very much awake. I want to see the lights in your eyes spark and shatter when you come.'

She gasped, her heart thudding like a drum in her chest at the pictures so vividly thrown up into her mind's eye. And once again she felt herself drowning under the waves of desire, lust and all things sensual. Unable to breathe or think or make sense of where she was.

Able only to feel.

And the fear welled up inside that soon she would have no choice; that maybe it was already too late.

'I'm afraid,' she admitted. 'It's too soon.'

'You want me,' he said, his mouth once again on hers, coaxing her into complicity, convincing her that this was the best way. The only way. 'It's not too soon to know that.'

He might be right, but still she wavered, because she had seen her sister give in to passion and take what she wanted of a man, had seen her left with his child and nothing else.

She did not want that for herself. She did not want a fleeting affair that might rapidly turn from lust to resentment or worse. She did not want a marriage that could turn so quickly empty, and from where she could not simply walk away.

She wanted the real deal. She didn't know how that was possible now, but that didn't stop her from wanting it. She had held on to that dream for too long to give up on it completely.

'It's not that easy,' she whispered against his stubbled jaw. 'I can't just—'

'Of course you can,' he soothed, his hot mouth stealing her words and making magic to convince her it would be the easiest thing in the world. 'I am a man, you are a woman and we want each other. What else matters?'

His hand scooped down her back, squeezing her behind, his fingers so perilously close to her heated core. She knew she must tell him or she would be on her back before he found out. She did not want him to find out that way. She could not bear it.

'Then maybe there is one more thing you should know,' she said, looking uncertainly up at him, feeling herself colour even as she spoke the words, 'because I have never done this before.'

The side of his mouth turned up, and the eyes that had so recently been molten with heat turned flat and hard. 'If you're still trying to get out of this, Princess, you should know I am not as gullible as my half-brother.'

CHAPTER TEN

HE SAW her flinch and caught the hurt in her eyes before she shoved herself away from him. He let her go, watched her putting distance between them as disbelief bloomed and grew large in his gut. A virgin? There was no way it could be true. 'You can't be serious. You're how old? And your sister...'

She spun around. 'Oh, of course! Because I'm twenty-four, and because my sister has two illegitimate children, then I must have slept with any number of men and somehow got lucky and escaped the same fate? How many men did you think, Zoltan? A dozen? One hundred? How many men did you think had broken down the gates and paved the way for your irresistible advances?'

'Princess,' he said. '*Aisha*, I never thought—'

'Of course you did. You didn't believe me before when I told you why Mustafa had not touched me. You thought it was some kind of joke. Well, the joke's well and truly on you. And if I had my way, even though we are married already, the gods would surely curse you as I now do.' Then she turned and strode away down the beach.

He watched her go, adding his own curses and feeling the effect of hers already. What a fool! He'd had her in the palm of his hand, supple and willing, so close to exploding she was like unstable dynamite. If only he'd reacted to her confession by telling her he'd be gentle with her, or that he thought her all the more precious for it—as he would have, if he'd thought for a moment she was speaking the truth—then she would have been his.

And that *should* have been his reaction, given what she had told him earlier. But back then he'd heard her story and had seen in it only the chance to laugh at Mustafa's stupidity. Because that was what he'd wanted to see.

He hadn't considered her in any part of it.

But then, he had never considered her.

He'd only seen what he had to do to satisfy the terms of an arrangement he'd had no part in making. He'd only wanted to grind his half-brother down to the nothing that he was in the process.

He was a fool, on so many counts. He'd been the stupid one.

As for Aisha? She was indeed a goddess.

A virgin goddess.

He watched her walk towards the camp as long as he could along the dark stretch of beach, watched until her flapping abaya was swallowed up by the night. Only then did he look up at the silvery moon and stars and feel the weight of his obligations sit heavily on his shoulders, feel the watchful eyes of the gods looking down on him, no doubt laughing at this sad and pitiful mortal who threw away destiny when it was handed to him on a platter.

And what to do? For she must be his wife in all senses of the word in time for the coronation if he was to become king, and there was one more night for that to happen.

That should be his most pressing imperative. But right now he wondered, for right now he was faced with choices he'd never seen coming.

He could have the kingdom and a wife he lusted after but who might hate him for ever if he took her before she was ready. Or he could have a wife who wanted him but who might take her own sweet time falling into his bed, in which case the kingdom might well in the meantime fall into the hands of a man he hated more than anyone.

And, when his duty to his country had been his prime motivating force until now, why was that suddenly such a difficult choice?

He slept badly that night. But how could he not when he'd lain awake not ten feet away from her all night? He'd heard her toss and turn through the night, he'd heard her muffled, despairing sighs and pillow punches when it was clear sleep was evading her too despite the gentling sounds of the sea on the shore. He'd registered the exact moment her breath had steadied and calmed and then he'd listened to the sounds of her sleeping. And all the time he thought about the waste of night hours and what they could have been doing if only he hadn't been such a damned fool.

When he rose early, he tried not to dwell too much on how good she looked asleep with her hair rippling over the pillow, or how easy it would be to climb into bed with her and finish this thing now. Except that she would truly hate him then, and somehow he didn't want her to hate him any more. If she could like him, even just a little, it would make this whole thing so much easier.

But he took one look at the table under his palms

waiting for him to resume his studies and baulked. He
had a problem to contend with and there was no space
in his head for study. Besides, there was still way too
much tension in his body to sit there quietly and take
anything in, tension he needed to work off to give himself the headspace to think. He looked out at the ocean,
inviting and calm, but swimming would involve going
back to the tent to change. Besides, the thought of
swimming made him think about her, looking lush and
edible in that citrus-coloured swimsuit, and he needed
to untangle his thoughts if he was to work out what he
was to do, not scramble them completely.

And she was more than capable of scrambling his
mind.

Already he was half-tempted by the thought of giving her as much time as she needed to fall into his bed.
But that would mean leaving the door open for Mustafa,
and how could he do that to Al-Jirad? How could he so
callously evade his duty?

But, for a prize like her, it would be almost worth
giving up the throne.

He shook his head, though he knew it would take
more than that to clear it. He heard the nicker of horses
and swung his head around.

Perfect.

Zoltan was nowhere to be seen when she rose, her head
feeling as if someone was pounding inside her skull
trying to break their way out. She could not remember
a worse night. But then, she had not had much experience of sharing a tent with a man who simultaneously
drove her wild with passion one minute, and so foaming with fury the next. And somewhere in the midst of
those extremes she felt a strange hurt, a sadness, that

things had gone so very wrong. But she would not dwell on how cheated she felt that they had not made love last night, or how her body had refused to relax, remaining so achingly high-strung half the night. She would not dwell on that at all.

Rani bringing her tea was just the distraction she needed. If she was going to worry, it might as well be about something important, and someone must have heard from Marina by now. 'Is there any news of my sister this morning?' she asked as the steam from the fragrant, spiced liquid curled in the air.

'No news, mistress.'

For the first time, Aisha felt a prickly discomfort about her sister's failure to arrive. Sure, Marina might be headstrong and wayward, and abhor anything to do with the constraints of convention, but why would she not attend her sister's marriage, and now the coronation? Surely she would attend for her sister's sake, at least?

'The master is riding, Princess,' Rani continued, breaking into her thoughts. 'Would you like a horse prepared for you?'

Aisha almost said no. Almost. But then she thought about riding along the beach, the wind in her hair, the closest she would ever get to being free again, and the idea held such appeal that she agreed. Maybe it might even blow away this growing concern in her gut that Marina hadn't shown up. Maybe it might make her see that her sister was just making a statement that she disapproved of this marriage and its terms and she was staying away as a protest. *Maybe.*

'Which way did Sheikh Zoltan go?' she asked when her horse was brought to her a few minutes later. When the groom pointed one way down the beach, she pointed her mount the other way.

* * *

It had been worth visiting the rest of the tribes people, Zoltan thought as he neared the point, taking a circular route back to the camp. Talking with them had made his path clearer and shown him what was needed. Al-Jirad had progressed in many areas under the rule of King Hamra, but there were still advances to be made in education and healthcare delivery, especially for these wandering people.

It was clear he should thank Aisha for breaking the ice and putting him in contact with them. He would not have thought to visit them otherwise.

It was also clear that he could not entrust the future of anyone, let alone his people, to the likes of Mustafa. That man did not want the throne of Al-Jirad for any reason other than his own personal aggrandisement. He cared nothing for the people.

Strange, he mused as his mount nimbly negotiated the rocky shoreline, how quickly he had come to think of the people of Al-Jirad as his people. He had taken on this role begrudgingly out of a sense of duty, and because the alternative was too ugly a prospect to entertain. He had taken it on all the while resenting the changed direction it meant for his life, and the loss of a business he had created from the ground up, the biggest and best executive-jet leasing business in the world. He had been only months away from achieving that goal when he had taken the call and realised he could not do both. Where was his resentment now? Where was his anger? Instead he felt a kind of pride that he was able to follow in his beloved uncle's footsteps. He would honour King Hamra's memory by being a good king.

The coronation must proceed.

Which meant he could not wait for Aisha to make up her mind. They would have to consummate the marriage before the coronation, which meant he would have to go back to the camp and explain, once again, that she had no choice. But after the mess he had made last night, he just hoped he could word it in a way she would understand. She *had* to understand.

It was duty, pure and simple, after all.

Except, thinking about it, his groin already tightening, maybe this part was not so much duty...

He saw her as he rounded the point, probably one hundred metres down the beach. He stopped for a moment to watch her gallop along the shore, her long hair flying behind her, the hem of her abaya flapping in the wind, the rest of it plastered against her body as spray from the horse's hooves scattered like jewels around her, and he realised the word 'goddess' came nowhere close to describing her.

Then she saw him, and he lifted one hand in greeting, but she pulled her horse up and turned before galloping in the other direction.

So she was still angry with him about last night, he thought as he set off in pursuit. Not entirely unexpected, but nevertheless not a good start when she was probably only going to get angrier with what he had to tell her.

His stallion powered down the shore. She was a good horsewoman and she had a decent head start, but her horse was nowhere near as big or as powerful as his and steadily his stallion narrowed the lead until they were galloping side by side across the sand.

She glanced across at him and dug her heels into her mount's flank. It responded with a spurt of speed but it was no trouble for his powerful horse to catch her. 'We need to talk,' he shouted into the air between them.

'I have nothing to talk to you about.'

'It's important.'

'Go to hell!'

'Listen to me.'

'I hate you!'

And she wheeled her horse around and took off the other way. He pulled his mount to a halt, its mouth foaming, nostrils snorting as he watched her go.

'You want a race, Princess,' he muttered into the air as he geed the horse into pursuit. 'You've got one.'

He was gaining on her again. She knew he would, she knew she couldn't escape him for ever, but he wasn't even supposed to have come this way. And she didn't want to talk. She didn't want to have to listen to him. She didn't even want to see him. How dared he look so good on a horse, with his white shirt flapping against his burnished skin, looking like some kind of bandit? How dared he?

She glanced over her shoulder, saw him just behind and urged her mount faster.

Barbarian!

All night he had lain there as if she didn't exist, as if he didn't care that she was hurt and upset and angry. All that time he had made not one attempt to try to make up for what he had done. Not even one. He had let her lie there waiting for him to do—something—and he had done precisely nothing. He had let her lie there aching and burning and he had made not one move to comfort her.

Bastard!

'Aisha,' he called, alongside her once again. 'Stop!'

He reached across, snatched the reins out of her hands and pulled the two horses to a halt.

She shrieked and smacked at his hand and realised it was useless, so she slid off the saddle, swiping at the tears streaming down her face. She splashed through the shallows, her abaya wet and slapping against her legs, tiny fish panicking and darting every which way before her frantic splashing feet.

She did not even know why she was crying, only that now the tears had started she didn't know how to turn them off.

'Aisha!'

She felt his big hands clamp down on her shoulders, she felt the brake of his body and his raw, unsuppressed heat, and she sobbed, hating him all the more for reducing her to this. 'Leave me alone!'

But he did not leave her alone. He turned her in his hands and she closed her eyes so she could not see his face. There was nothing but silence stretching taut and thin between them. And just when she could not stand it any more, just when she was sure he must be enjoying this moment so very, very much, he crushed her to his chest. 'Oh, Aisha, what have I done? What have I done?'

If he hadn't been holding her, she would have collapsed in tears in the shallows.

Instead she sobbed hard against the wall of his chest.

'Aisha,' he said, one hand stroking her head, the other behind her, holding her to him, 'I do not deserve you. I am afraid I will never deserve you.' He cradled her head in his hand and she felt the press of his mouth on the top of her head; felt the crush of her breasts against his chest; felt the stirrings of unrequited need build again, as if they had been lying in wait for just such an opportunity, ready to resume their pulsing insistence.

'Can you ever, ever forgive me for the way I have treated you?'

She sniffed. His shirt was sodden against her face. 'I don't want to forgive you,' she whispered against his

skin, afraid to pull her face away. Afraid to look at him.
'I want to hate you.'

There was another achingly long pause and this time
she was sure the thin wire connecting them would snap
before he answered. 'I don't want to be hated.'

'I can't,' she said, releasing another flood of tears.
'I want to. I've tried, but I can't. And I hate you for it.'

He laughed then, no more than a rumble in his chest,
and she wanted to hit him for being able to find hu-
mour where there was none—until he said, 'You do
not know what a relief that is. I don't think I have ever
heard more wondrous words in my life.' He lifted her
chin between his fingers and she resisted at first, hating that he was seeing her like this, tear-streaked and
swollen-eyed. But his persuasive fingers had their way,
and she blinked up at him, saw his dark eyes upon her,
the dark features of his face so—tortured.

'I could never live with myself if you hated me,
Aisha, even though I know I deserve it, even though I
have made such a mess of this. Can you ever, even in
some tiny way, forgive me?'

The tears welled anew. She sniffed. He leant down
and kissed first one eye, and then the other. 'I do not
enjoy knowing that I make you cry.'

She pressed her lips together, her skin tingling where
his lips had pressed. He leant down and kissed the end
of her nose. And, in spite of herself, she jagged up her
chin so her nose butted up harder against his lips, wanting the contact, needing more.

His hands grew suddenly warmer around her, scooping down lower and less soothing, more *appreciative*;
the air around them was suddenly super-charged and
electric and his dark eyes spoke of more than torture.

For in their dark depths she saw heat and desire and the promise of pleasure like she'd never known before.

'Aisha...'

And she knew before his head dipped that he intended to kiss her. She knew it and did not a thing to prevent it. Because it was what she wanted, this kiss with this man in this time.

His arms tightened around her as he drew her close. *'Aisha,'* he whispered in the second before their lips connected.

It was like coming home. It was like every time she'd been away from home and returned to the palace in Jemeya and felt its welcome warmth and familiarity wrap around her. It was just like that. Only one thousand times better.

For his kiss didn't just deliver familiarity. It offered a new dimension. It promised pleasures unbound.

And as she feasted on his hot mouth, and fed from the magic dance of his lips and tongue, all she knew was that she wanted all of those pleasures and she wanted them now. She could all but taste them.

She groaned into his mouth, her hands clutching at his shirt, fisting in the fine cotton as his hands cupped her behind and pulled her close, pulled her hard against the long, hot heat of him. And this time, she knew, she would not be left waiting and wondering. This time she would discover the pleasures she had waited for all these years.

It would not be so bad, she told herself; she would not be giving up on her dream, merely recognising life had changed the parameters. It did not mean it could not still work eventually. And meanwhile...

Meanwhile she could not breathe. Someone had sucked the oxygen out of existence and all that was keeping her going was the heated sweep of his hands on her body, the molten lure of his mouth and the rigid promise of his erection. Those things fed into her own need and stoked the fire beneath her until she was red-hot and rabid with desire. Until she knew kissing was not enough.

'Please,' she begged. 'Please!'

He lifted his hot tongue from her throat. 'What do you want, my princess?'

And her hunger and desire coalesced into one indisputable fact. 'I want you, Zoltan. I want to feel you inside me.'

CHAPTER ELEVEN

SHE felt him lift his head from hers and look up to the sky. She heard his roar. She felt his triumph in hers. Because she knew she was right.

He carried her back to the camp as he had done that first night, in front of her on his stallion, but this time she was not wrapped in a cloak and bound to him. This time she clung to him herself, looking up at all the harsh angles and dark shadows of his face, wondering how she had never thought them beautiful before.

For he was. Darkly, supremely beautiful.

When they arrived back at the camp, he slid out of the saddle and reached up for her, taking her in his arms as if she were weightless and looking at her as if she were the only woman in the world.

She liked that look as he swung her down. At that moment she wanted to be the only woman in the world for him for ever. But this moment and how it made her feel would do, even if there was no other. Because surely it couldn't get better than this?

He carried her into the tent and pulled the flap closed, signalling they were not to be disturbed. She swallowed at that. Everyone outside would know what they were doing inside, yet instead of stultifying her somehow that only managed to heighten her excitement.

Then Zoltan was there in front of her again and there was no room to care about anyone else because there was only the two of them. He slid one hand behind her neck. 'You are so beautiful,' he said, and even though she knew he was being generous, that her kohl must be smudged and her eyes swollen from tears, the knowledge he could see past that fed into her very soul.

As did the assurance they were already married. He didn't have to impress her now. He didn't have to pretend. She was already his wife in name and he could take his time making her so in fact.

She was so grateful he hadn't pushed her. Maybe she might have taken longer to get to this stage if they hadn't already been married, but for now there was no reason to delay. This was the man she was wedded to. This was the man she was bound to.

And when she looked up at him, tall and broad and wanting her, it felt not such a bad place to be.

'Are you still scared?' he asked as he gathered her into his arms. She nodded, afraid to speak lest he hear the quake in her voice, before he said, 'Then I will do my best to make it as pleasurable as possible. I owe you that, at least.'

His hot mouth went to work on her to smooth her concerns away as he laid her reverently on the bed. He made no move to undress her, and she wanted to cry with relief, for she wasn't yet ready to bare everything to him. It felt so good, anyway. He made it feel so good.

He made *her* feel so good.

She liked the way he kissed, giving her all he had to give. Their mouths meshed, his tongue inviting hers into the dance. She liked the way his hands skimmed her body, curving over a hip or cupping a breast, making her gasp when his thumb flicked over a sensitive nipple.

She liked the way his body felt under her hands. Firm. Strong. Sculpted.

Except she was too hot and he was wearing too many clothes. Way too many clothes. She pulled his shirt from his trousers so she could slide her hands up the bare skin of his back, relishing the feel of skin against skin, only it was not nearly enough to satisfy her.

And all the while the need inside her built, the heat inside her escalated. She felt as if she was losing herself, drowning under a wave of sensations, but wanting more, driven to find more.

He gave her more.

His mouth dipped to her breast, his hot tongue laving at her nipple, and she gasped as heat met need in a rush that sent sensation spearing through her, a direct line from breast to her heated core.

She was way too hot, and if his hand hadn't already been at her knee, smoothing her abaya up from her legs, she would have ripped it off herself. His hand scooped higher, deliciously higher, as his mouth wove magic at her breast and she wound her fingers through his hair hoping that he would pause, *there*, where her need was so great.

But he did not pause. She whimpered a little as he moved on and drew her gown higher over her belly. He lifted his mouth now, so that he could slip her gown higher, his fingers trailing sparks under her skin, or so it seemed. She unwound her arms and he eased the gown over her head and rocked back on his knees, looking down at her in just her underwear, drinking her in from her toes to her eyes, looking at her in a way that banished her fears that he might find fault with her now when she was so close, that put a fire under her blood.

'You are beautiful, Princess,' he said as he unbuttoned his shirt. 'You are perfection.'

His voice was so thick and tight that it was like gravel against her senses. His dark eyes were almost black, and brimming with need.

She knew little of love-making apart from what she had read in books, but she knew that it must be taking too long because this need inside her burned so hot!

'I want you,' she said, wanting him to know that in case he was taking his time because he thought she might yet change her mind. He growled deep in his throat, tore the shirt from his shoulders and undid the buckle of his belt. She watched, transfixed, as his busy, clever hands worked the trousers undone, watched hungrily as he slid them over his hips and kicked them aside.

She gazed at his masculine beauty, at the perfection of his form, at the bulge in his underwear, before he joined her once again on the bed, scooping her back into his arms.

Skin brushed by the cooling air was now brushed with the smooth of his hand and with his heated lips. He kissed her lips, nose and eyes, he trailed kisses down her throat, took her hand and kissed his way up her arm, her wrist, the inside of her elbow and down the other.

He didn't so much kiss her as worship her body, and when he dispensed with her bra she let it go with no protest. Why would she protest when her breasts wanted his mouth on them with no barrier between them?

His tongue took a wicked trail across her belly and it was almost too much, her body never more alive, never more on fire. And then his hand cupped her mound and her spine arched into the bed. 'Please,' she begged.

'What do you want, Princess?'

'I want you,' she gasped. 'Inside me.'

Laughter rumbled from him and into her as his mouth found her thigh and he proceeded to kiss his way down one leg.

Why was he taking so damned long? Her hands fisted in the covers as she was driven wild with desire, wild with need. She needed him inside her, and he was raining kisses on her instep.

'Someone is impatient,' he said as she kicked at him, urging him on.

'Haven't I waited long enough?' she came back with, her chest heaving, pulling her leg away.

'But if you have waited this long, surely a few more minutes won't matter?'

'I might die before then,' she replied and threw her head back into the pillows as he kissed his way up her inner thigh. 'Oh God.'

'Do you like that?'

'Mmm,' she managed. He must have been listening because she felt his fingers trace the waistline of her lace panties, felt them sneak under and scoop them down, felt his hands gentle her legs apart.

Oh God.

Every cell in her body tensed and clamped shut. This was it!

It was, and yet it wasn't, for in one shocked moment she realised his head was still between her thighs. 'You can't,' she said, then he parted her and she felt the sweep of his tongue against her inner lips and she almost cried out with the utter pleasure of it—did cry out when she felt his tongue circle that tiny, concentrated nub of nerve endings.

Already she was lost. She was panting now, lost in a new world with no idea how to find her way out and with no wish to find her way out any time soon. Not until she found this magical place he was taking her.

She hated him for making her wait, for delivering such exquisite torture, hated him and loved him for making her feel so very much.

Just when she thought she could not take any more, she felt his fingers upon her, circling her very core, working in train with his busy lips and tongue. One finger pressed inside her and her muscles clamped down at the invasion. But it was hardly unwanted. A swish of his tongue and she sighed and relaxed, only to feel another push into her alongside it.

Suddenly it was too much. There was too much to enjoy. Too much pleasure. She felt that pleasure spiral upwards, felt her whole being reduced to sensation, and then with a final flick of his clever tongue and press of his fingers inside her she was sent catapulting into the sky.

He held her while she rocked back to earth. He pressed kisses to her belly and breasts and lips where she tasted herself on his mouth.

'But you…' she managed, feeling as limp as a rag doll.

'Think you're amazing.'

And some part of her that still registered compliments glowed. She had done nothing and he could still say that? She sensed him rise up, heard the swish of fabric over skin and opened her eyes to see him between her legs, his hand guiding his erection towards her. So large. So alive and wondrous.

'You're so beautiful,' she whispered in awed reverence. 'Do you think…?'

'Oh,' he said, leaning down to suck her into his kiss, 'I know.'

She tasted his mouth on hers then, felt it tug her into his world, convincing her with the persuasive play of his tongue and losing her until with a start she realised he was there, butting and straining against her entrance. Even when she panicked, his hand was there below her to lift her and ease the angle.

But he was there, *right there*, and she would have panicked but he was also right there with her, taking her higher again with his kiss. Suddenly a pressure became a presence and, with a flash of pain that went as quickly as it had come, he was inside her.

She stilled then, stunned by what had happened, feeling his fullness deep within her body. He was inside her and, now the moment of pain had gone, she felt only that amazing sensation. But was that it? Was this how it was supposed to be?

He kissed her eyes. 'Are you all right?' She blinked up at him, seeing his concern in the tiny creases around his eyes, and she knew she loved him, just a little, even then. He shifted his elbows, a movement that shifted his body subtly so very far below and she gasped at the unexpected friction.

'I'm good,' she said. 'You *feel* so good.'

He growled at that and raised his hips, and she felt the sliding loss of him even as muscles she'd never realised she possessed battled to hang on.

He thrust back into her, this time with greater force. Why had she never done this? she wondered as her head was driven back into the pillows. Why had she waited when the pleasure was so exquisite, so addictive?

Then he withdrew and thrust into her again and she knew why—because she had wanted to save herself for the one who was special, the one who could make her feel this good. Zoltan made her feel this good.

Zoltan was the one.

She had saved herself for the very best.

And with every thrust of his hips she knew that to be true; with every thrust of his hips she knew she would never find a higher place.

But she found it now, when the slide of him inside her turned incendiary, and she combusted in a shattering explosion that featured the sun, moon and stars.

It could have ended there, but she heard his roar, felt his shuddering climax, and it drove her still further through the galaxies until he launched her again into nothingness and the sky gave way to the glow of a tiny kernel of knowledge.

She loved him.

Something had shifted the sands beneath his feet. Something had shifted the foundations of his very world while he wasn't looking.

Something?

Or *someone*?

For, while Zoltan's body pulsed with the post-release hum as he lay back against the pillows, his breathing slowly steadying, his mind grappled with the impossible. She was perfect in every way. How could she be? Yet she had responded instinctively to his every move, naturally and sometimes even wantonly, despite being uneducated and unrehearsed, and her unskilled reactions had stoked the fire raging inside him, higher and higher, until he had even felt himself consumed.

When had that ever happened before?

How could she, a virgin before this night, do such a thing? He had expected to pleasure her, to make this coupling as easy as possible. Never had he expected that he would find paradise himself.

He turned to her, touched the fingers of one hand to the line of her cheek, wanting to put into words how he felt but unsure how to go about it, surprised when he felt moisture there. He sat up. 'Did I hurt you?'

She shook her head, blinking away the tears. 'I had no idea. I didn't know it could be that good.'

'Usually it's not,' he said, sliding one arm beneath her. Then, because some part of him realised that honesty could be couched in better terms, he went on. 'It's never been that good for me. Never before.' She looked up at him, her dark eyes wide and a tiny frown between her brows, as if wondering whether to believe him or not. Suddenly she shuddered in his arms and her eyes and lips squeezed shut, a woman battling to keep control.

'Aisha,' he said, smoothing her brow with his free hand as tears insisted on squeezing past her closed lids, 'I did hurt you. I'm sorry. I was trying to be gentle.'

She shook her head, tried to turn away, but he gathered her closer into the circle of his arms. 'No. I was thinking about Mustafa and what he said he'd do to me. Zoltan, if you had not come I would still be there. If you had not saved me, it would be him in my bed. It would be him...' She shook her head. 'Oh God, it would be him in my bed.'

He tried to gentle her with his hands as his own heart grew weightier in his chest. 'He cannot hurt you now,'

'He would have.' She sniffed back on the threat of more tears. 'He had an old woman examine me,' she said, her voice thready and thin. 'He wouldn't believe me until she had poked and prodded and confirmed what I had told him. Only then he believed. Only then he left me alone.'

Her voice cracked on the last word and this time

she dissolved into tears. He pulled her in, cradled her head against his chest and let her cry, her tears ripping at his soul.

He did not deserve her thanks. She had been right all along—he was a barbarian. He—who knew Mustafa better than anyone—had paid no heed to what she must have suffered at his half-brother's hands. He had seen her rescue as a way of evening the score between them. And once she had been in his hands he had asked her nothing. He had demanded everything.

Worst of all, he had not believed her.

He was no better than his half-brother and that knowledge tore at his gut. He dropped his head to hers, pressed his lips to her hair. 'I am so sorry, Aisha, that I did not believe you. I was so wrong.'

He lifted her tear-streaked face to his, kissed her damp eyes and the tip of her nose. 'Can you ever forgive me for the way I have treated you?'

She blinked up at him, her soft lips parted, looking so lost and vulnerable, so very kissable, that he felt the kick all the way down in his groin. She gave a tentative smile, touched a slim hand to his chest and down his side, her fingers curling deliciously into the flesh of his buttock. 'Maybe,' she said hesitantly, taking his hand, putting it to her breast, her eyelids fluttering closed as his hand cupped her breast, his thumb stroking her nipple.

'Anything,' he said as she set both her hands on him, exploring, tracing every detail, setting his skin alight, turning his voice to gravel. 'Name it.'

'Make me forget him. Make love to me again. I mean, when it is possible.'

He growled low in his throat and, still holding onto her, flipped onto his back so she straddled him, his eyes drinking in the sight of her rising up from him, his hands drinking in her satin-smooth skin.

'Oh,' she said, her eyes widening as she realised he was already primed beneath her, 'I thought it would be too soon.'

'No,' he said as he encouraged her hips higher so he could position himself, loving the way she so naturally assisted with the movement of her lush body to find her centre. 'With you, Aisha,' he said, as he drew her down his long length, 'anything is possible.'

CHAPTER TWELVE

For the first time in days she felt that things were finally going right and falling into place. They had woken in the tent to the sound of waves breaking on the shore. They had made slow, lazy love as the sun had risen over the horizon. They had held hands while travelling across the sands to the Blue Palace.

And now, sitting in the front row of the Blue Palace's magnificent twelfth-century arched reception hall, grandly fitted out for the coronation of Al-Jirad's new king, she felt not only happiness but immense pride as well.

For in front of her stood Zoltan, now only minutes from being crowned King of Al-Jirad. The building was full of assembled guests from countries near and far, and her father sat alongside, beaming widely, no doubt at the knowledge he would be keeping his crown and that the Jemeyan legacy and the pact between their two countries would live on.

As for Aisha? She was so full of the new wonders of love-making that she could not begin to describe how she felt: glowing. Buzzing. Electric, with a heightened awareness of all things of the flesh. For Zoltan had awakened in her the pleasures of the flesh in a way she had never dreamed possible. She smiled to herself, thinking of the latest way he'd pleasured her—asking her to don the gossamer-thin robe she'd been gifted, pleasuring her with his clever tongue and seeking lips before taking her again. Was there no end to his talents?

Not so far, apparently.

He had told her that with her all things were possible. Could it be true? Could they find love out of the madness of a forced marriage neither of them had wanted? Might Zoltan grow to love her as she so wished to be loved?

Last night he had made it seem possible.

Only one thing could temper her joy this day and it was that there was still no word from Marina. She tried to tell herself not to be surprised—it was Marina, after all, and she had never been one for protocol and obligations, especially when it involved anything remotely connected to duty. But still, after all that had happened, Aisha had so very much wanted to have the chance to talk to her sister again.

Around her the formalities dragged on longer than she expected, and she zoned out, listening with only half an ear. It was not entirely intentional, but there was only so much pomp and ceremony one could take in when one had other, much more carnal pleasures on their mind, and right now she had the memories of last night's activities to savour as well as the upcoming night's activities to anticipate.

And there was really no need to listen. It was all just a formality, after all. And it was all so long…

Until she heard the name of her island home mentioned, and the pact. She blinked into awareness and she realised why the ceremony was taking so long, because an extra segment had been added to the ceremony due to the unusual circumstances of the ascension, a series of declarations Zoltan was required to respond to.

'And do you solemnly swear,' the Grand Vizier said, 'on the covenants of the Sacred Book of Al-Jirad that you have married a Jemeyan princess?'

She glanced from her father to Zoltan, not knowing she would be mentioned as part of this, and suddenly wishing she'd paid more attention, for neither of them looked surprised or perplexed.

'I declare it to be true,' Zoltan said.

'And do you also solemnly swear, on the covenants of the Sacred Book of Al-Jirad, that you have impregnated with your seed the Jemeyan princess you have married so that Al-Jirad and Jemeya might both prosper into the future just as your family will prosper?'

'I declare it to be true.'

'Then you have fulfilled the covenants of the Sacred Book of Al-Jirad and I declare…'

But Aisha heard nothing more. For her blood had turned to ice and the thunder of it in her ears drowned out the proceedings while her mind focused on the words *you have impregnated with your seed the Jemeyan princess*…

He had been *required* to impregnate her before the ceremony take place, as part of his requirements to become king?

The blood in her veins grew even colder. Was that what their trip away to Belshazzah had really been about, even while he had told her it was merely to get to know each other better?

For he must have known he would need to sleep with her before the coronation. The vizier would have told him.

He must have known.

Yet he hadn't told her. He'd let her think that it didn't matter how long it took, so long as they were married and gave the impression of sleeping together.

He'd let her think that she could take her time to get to know him.

He'd let her think she had a choice.

But he had known!

All the time he had known. She thought back to their time at Belshazzah, and to the skilfull way he had given her space and then reeled her in again, like a fisherman playing a fish. Giving it line, letting it think it was free, only to reel it back before letting it run again. He'd done the same with her, letting her think she had space, letting her walk alone, letting her make choices. But she'd been on a line all along and he'd known that all he had to do was reel her in and *impregnate* her.

She shuddered at the very sound of the word. It sounded so cold, formal and clinical. It sounded a million miles from what she thought they had been doing that day.

And all the time he had let her believe that it had meant something.

What had he told her? *It's never been that good for me.* She had wondered then whether he was telling her the truth, wanting in her heart to believe it but so scared to.

He had wanted her to believe it too. So she would become the biddable, complicit wife he needed.

And she had wanted so much to believe him. When would she learn?

She felt sickened, physically ill, and when she gasped in air to quell the sudden unwanted surge of her stomach her father frowned across at her and she did her best to send a reassuring smile back in his direction. It would

not be the done thing for a Jemeyan princess to throw
up at her own husband's coronation.

Somehow she made it through to the end of the ceremony, avoiding eye-contact as she placed her arm on
his, stiff and formal, as the royal party departed.

Somehow her legs managed to carry her all the way
from the ceremony to the balcony of the palace.

Somehow she even managed to smile stiffly at the
crowd gathered in the square spread out below to cel-
ebrate their first sight of the new King and Queen of
Al-Jirad.

Their cheers didn't come close to touching her. The
only word she heard over and over in her mind was
impregnate.

'You seem tense, Aisha.'

'Do I?'

She had suffered through the interminable state reception, putting up with inane small-talk and diplomatic
and ultimately meaningless mutterings with as much
grace as she could muster. But now, as she removed
one of the heavy chandelier earrings from her lobe, she
could enjoy a brief respite in their suite as they changed
before a formal dinner.

Or she could have enjoyed it, that was, if Zoltan
hadn't also been there. She pulled the other earring
loose and dropped it to the dressing table in a clatter,
just wanting the heavy weight gone from her ear, and
wishing that the heavy weight on her heart could be so
easily discarded.

Across the room Zoltan stopped tugging at his tie. 'It
appears the stress of becoming queen is getting to you.'

'Tell me about it.'

'So maybe you need to relax.'

'And what did you have in mind?' she said, the taste of bile bitter in her throat. 'Perhaps a little *impregnation* to calm me down and turn me back into your oh-so-biddable wife?'

He blinked. Slowly. His jaw set. 'Is that what you're upset about, the wording of the ceremony?' He shrugged. 'It's ancient. It is required by the texts.'

'As, it seems, was the need to *impregnate* me before the coronation.'

'Aisha,' he said, coming closer, putting his hands to her shoulders, 'don't be like this.'

'Don't touch me!' she said, brushing his hands away. 'You knew, didn't you? You knew before we went to Belshazzah that you had to get me to sleep with you.'

'Princess,' he said, holding out one hand to her. 'Aisha, what is the point of this? It is already done. Did you not enjoy it?'

Her chest heaving with indignation at his inference that everything must be all right if the sex was any good, she demanded, 'What would have happened if you had not impregnated me before the coronation? If your answer to that question in the ceremony had been no?'

His jaw ground together, his eyes glinted. 'I would not have been crowned king.'

'And you knew that all the time we were at Belshazzah.'

'I knew.'

'And not once did you bother to tell me.'

'I tried. I was going to—'

'I don't believe you!'

'It's the truth! I was going to—'

'No! You told me you were taking me there so we might get to know each other, because the palace was too big, too public. You never once told me it was so you could secure the throne by ensuring I slept with you in time for the coronation. Don't you remember what you told me in the car on the way, that you didn't need to go to so much trouble to get into my pants because you could so easily find a dark corner in the palace to perform the task?'

'"Getting into your pants" are your words. They were never mine.'

'Don't get semantic, because playing with words won't work in this case. It doesn't matter which words you use. Because when it all comes down to it that's what you needed, that's what you wanted, wasn't it? Getting into my pants—impregnating me with your seed—only that would ensure you the throne.'

'I never lied to you,' he said, 'just because I didn't tell you the intimate details of the pact.'

She scoffed, indignant at the way he could worm his way around the truth. 'Not openly, perhaps. You didn't tell me what you knew. Instead you let me think that sleeping with you was my choice, that I had some say. While all the time you knew the clock was already ticking.

'Your lie was a lie all the same. It was one of omission.'

'Princess. Aisha, listen.'

'No! I am through with listening to you. Do you have any idea how betrayed I feel right now? How shattered that you could not entrust me with the details of my own future?' She put her shaking head in her hands before she raised her head and flung her arms wide. 'No. I am done with it, just as I am done with you and anything to do with you.'

'What are you saying?'

'I'm saying I have had enough of this farce of a marriage. I want out of it.'

'You can't just walk away from this marriage. You are bound to me just as I am bound to you.'

'Why shouldn't I walk away? You're king now. You don't need me any more. Don't try to tell me that the Sacred Book of Al-Jirad, the font of all knowledge and power, would prevent a queen who has been lied to and manipulated from escaping the chains of her captives? I am sure the wisdom of the ages would be on her side. And, if not, I am sure the weight of modern justice would support her.'

'Even though you have not yet finished your duty? You have yet to deliver the necessary heirs expected of this union.'

She tossed her head. 'Who knows, maybe there is a little bastard prince already implanted in my womb.'

'We are married. He would not be a bastard.'

'You don't think so?' From somewhere she managed to dredge up a smile. 'Though maybe you're right. Maybe he won't take after you. In any event, I am not staying here in this place a moment longer. I am going home to Jemeya.'

'You forget something, Princess—you need to supply two heirs.'

She raised her chin. 'So send me your sperm, Zoltan, and I will gladly save you any more pretence and any more of your lies and I will happily *impregnate* myself!'

He'd always known she was shallow. Zoltan crashed through the air as he strode down the passageway towards his suite, sick of a night spent making excuses, tired of explaining the new queen was unfortunately 'indisposed'.

She wasn't indisposed. What he'd really wanted to tell people was that she was a spoilt little princess who wanted everything all her own way—expected it—as if it was her God-given right. Well, he'd never wanted this marriage in the first place himself. He was better off without her. He would cope just fine. He tugged at the button at his collar, needing more oxygen than the suddenly tight collar allowed.

But—damn—maybe not Al-Jirad.

He would have to talk to Hamzah, find out how the queen's sudden absence would change things, to see if there was a workable way around her absence. There was nothing he could recall in the Sacred Book of Al-Jirad, but Hamzah would know the legalities of it all. Although her father would no doubt talk her around eventually; he was as hard-nosed about doing one's duty as anyone when it all came down to it. He had promised Zoltan tonight when they had exchanged a quiet word earlier on that he would soon talk sense into his precious daughter's head.

Wall hangings fluttered as he passed like a dark storm cloud, creating turbulence in the formerly serene air.

And the thing that made him angrier than ever, the thing that made him steam and fume, was that for just one day, just a few short hours, he had actually believed that this marriage might work.

He'd actually believed they had something that could take this marriage beyond the realms of duty and into something entirely more pleasurable.

Fool!

He'd been blinded by sex, pure and simple. So blown away by the delights of her sweet, responsive body, he'd forgotten what he was dealing with: a skin-deep princess who wanted the entire fairy-tale, from the once-upon-a-time to the happy-ever-after. When was she going to realise this was real life, not the pages from some child's picture book?

He paused as he came to the door of her suite, wondering if she'd already had her belongings removed and shipped. Nothing would surprise him.

He pushed open the door. It was silent inside and eerily dark with the closed curtains, only the light from the still-open door spilling in. There was no trace of her. He crossed the floor to her dressing room and tugged open the door. Nothing. She'd had them pack every single thing and wasted no time about it. They had taken every trace, until one might think she had never been here at all.

He ground his teeth together as he contemplated her mood when she had given the instructions to collect her belongings. Clearly she did not consider her return to Jemeya to be in any way temporary. Clearly she had no wish to be here. Maybe he should cut his losses and let her go. He would be well rid of her. He would have to ask Hamzah if that was an option that could be tolerated.

He was on his way out when his passing caused something to flutter, like loose papers riffling in the breeze, and he turned towards where the sound had come from. He pulled open a curtain, let light flood in and found them straight away. There were some loose papers on a desk tucked haphazardly under a blotter. He frowned, remembering a letter she'd been writing the night they'd been married when he'd come looking for her; remembering the way her fingers had shifted the pages as she'd looked down at them. The rushed packers had not done such a thorough job after all.

He pulled them out, intending to fling them in the nearest bin, when her neat handwriting caught his eye. Of course she would have neat handwriting and not some scrawl, he thought, finding yet another reason to resent her. She had probably been tutored in perfect script from an early age.

He didn't intend to read any of it, but he caught the words 'foolish' and 'naive' and he thought she must be talking about him, compiling a list of his faults.

That would be right. She had sat here on her wedding night and made a list of his failings—and to her sister, no less. No wonder it was such a long letter.

So what did his little princess really think of him? This should be amusing.

But as he read it wasn't amusement he felt. It was not him she was calling a fool. It was herself, for wishing she could choose a marriage partner, for ever thinking that she might one day marry a man for love, a good man who would love her for who she really was.

A ball formed in his gut, hard and heavy. He knew he shouldn't read on, but he could not stop. And he felt sick, knowing he was not that man she had wished for, and knowing that she saw herself as flawed when life and circumstances had conspired against her, when he knew it wasn't life she should be blaming. For he was the one at fault, he was the man who had shattered her dreams.

And he still wasn't sure why he cared.

When had duty got tangled with desire? Maybe about the time he had realised she was who she had said she was—an innocent.

Or maybe about the time duty had tangled with need. *Aisha.*

All she had wanted was a man to love her the way

she should be loved. Those words had meant nothing to him before. Her hopes and wishes had been like so much water poured on sand, for they had been thrown together, strangers, and what did it matter what either of them wanted when neither of them had a choice?

But he knew her now, better than before, and seeing her thoughts written down so clearly, knowing how she'd been hurting all that time…

The ball in Zoltan's gut grew heavier, and heavier still as he saw her call herself naive for saving herself for some mythical and ultimately non-existent male, and as she apologised to her sister for all the times she'd thought Marina had tossed her virginity away lightly, because at least she'd chosen who she'd gifted it to. For it had been hers to give, and she'd been the one to make that decision, and now Aisha applauded her, even envied her, for she would never experience that privilege.

But beyond that she was sorry, she wrote, that she had ever considered herself something special for the choice she had made. A choice that had clearly backfired spectacularly.

The ball in Zoltan's gut grew spikes that tore at his vital organs.

She thought she wasn't special? She was the most special of them all.

A woman so perfect and pure that he had felt honoured that he had been the one to receive her precious gift.

Yet clearly that wasn't how she had felt. And, even though she had come willingly to him that night, ultimately she had had no choice. No wonder she felt so cheated and betrayed now. No wonder she had not hung around long enough for him to explain.

She had lost her most guarded possession to a barbar-

ian who had apparently taken it out of duty and purely
to satisfy the dusty requirement of some ancient covenants.

And now she was gone and all he was left with was
that memory. It killed him to realise that he had never
told her what that day had meant to him, had never put
into words how wondrous that experience had been.
He cursed himself that he had assumed she must have
known how he felt. For surely she must have known?

Why the hell hadn't he told her?

Why hadn't he thought to warn her of the ancient
declarations in the coronation ceremony before she
could imagine how he felt about what they had done,
that he had been merely impregnating her?

And he remembered her frosty demeanour, her shut-
down expression. He had wounded her so deeply. It de-
stroyed him to think he had hurt her and that she might
still be hurting.

He replaced the pages on the desk. He should not
have read as much as he had; in truth he should not have
read anything, but he was not sorry that he had. For
now he knew what he must do. He must go to Jemeya
and seek Aisha out. He must explain; he had to tell her
what he felt for her, he must seek her forgiveness. For
he had to get her back.

He had to.

Still, he wasn't sure why.

Only that he had to.

And from the mists of time he remembered those
words his uncle, the King, had told him, the only positive lesson from his youth that had stuck. 'Choose your
battles, and choose them wisely.'

He would go to her today. Tell her that he was sorry.
Ask her if she could trust him enough to give him one

more chance. Because this battle was worth fighting. This battle was one he could not afford to lose.

He could not let Aisha go. He could not bear the thought of her not being here with him.

Behind him the door was pushed open. 'Excellency,' the vizier uttered with relief, 'I have been looking for you everywhere. You must come quickly, there is news.'

For a heartbeat he hoped that Aisha had changed her mind and returned of her own accord.

'What is it?' he said.

'It's Mustafa,' the vizier said. 'He has taken Princess Marina hostage.'

Zoltan's blood ran cold.

As much as he hated his half-brother, his first thoughts went to his wife.

Aisha.

How would she feel when she learned the news? How terrified she would be, knowing what kind of man was holding her beloved sister.

Aisha had already suffered enough at the hands of his half-brother. She had suffered more at his own clumsy and ham-fisted efforts to possess her. He could not bear her to suffer more.

He would not allow it.

CHAPTER THIRTEEN

AISHA was sick with fear, sick with worry. Mustafa had Marina, had taken her hostage on her way to the coronation. Even though her father swore that she would be rescued and brought safely back to Jemeya to be reunited with her family, and despite the relief of learning that her two children were safe at home with their nanny, Aisha wondered when this nightmare would ever end.

The only positive thing that Aisha could see was that at least worrying about her sister took her mind off thinking about Zoltan.

Most of the time.

She picked up her childhood bear, from where it winked at her on its shelf, and hugged it, wandering to the window of her bedroom, the treasured bedroom she had yearned so desperately to return to. She looked out over the cliffs of her island home to the shoreline of Al-Jirad in the distance. For there lay another palace that stood encircled by sandy deserts ruled by a king she had once imagined she had felt something for.

Two days now she had been back in Jemeya, and she could not deny the truth any more, for each passing day piled a heavier weight on Aisha's heart than the one that had gone before. The fact Zoltan hadn't tried to stop her from leaving, the fact he had let her return to Jemeya in the first place—didn't that say something about how little he actually valued her as his wife? Didn't the fact he hadn't come after her speak for itself? Surely she had been right to leave when she had, no matter what her father had tried to tell her?

Two days. A world ago, it seemed now. And her time with Zoltan could almost be some kind of dream. Imaginary. Unimportant.

Except then she remembered the touch of heated hands and the brush of a whiskered cheek against her breast, the thrust of him deep inside her, and she knew that so long as the memories remained in her mind there was no way she could ever easily forget him.

Damn him.

Damn herself!

For now she was here, back in her own room where she had always maintained she wanted to be, and after the places he had taken her it seemed a hollow victory indeed.

A spoilt princess?

Maybe Zoltan had been right all along. For, yes, she still felt betrayed and manipulated, but when things hadn't gone her way she'd as good as stamped her feet and run away.

Fool.

She looked down at the bear in her arms. Maybe it was time she grew up. Maybe instead of sitting here locked away in her room, waiting for Zoltan to make a move, she should be the one to make an effort, to reach out with an olive branch. After all, they were married and bound together. They had slept together—made love together. And no matter what she had spat out in her anger to Zoltan, there was no way she did not want to feel his body between her thighs again.

Maybe, if that was to happen, it was time for her to reach out to him, and if he didn't want her back, well, she wasn't an inexperienced virgin with dreams of falling in love with the man of her dreams any more. She was a woman. She would cope with whatever happened.

But first she owed it to herself to try.

There was a commotion outside her room, raised voices and someone shouting her name, and then the door was flung open and her father burst through, the smile on his face a mile wide, and next to him, her beaming sister.

'Marina!' she cried, and flung herself into her open arms.

It was a noisy reunion, filled with laughter and tears of joy, and it was only when her father went off to order a feast that Aisha had the chance to draw Marina aside to talk. They curled their feet beneath them on a sofa overlooking the sea and held hands as they had done ever since they were children.

'I was so afraid,' Aisha confessed. 'Did he hurt you? Mustafa, I mean. He must have been so angry that he had lost me.'

Her sister patted her hand and for a moment her eyes grew serious, the muscles in her face tight. 'He was angry. And bitter. He delighted in telling me in how many ways he would have me.' Her eyebrows raised. 'And in great detail.'

Aisha shuddered, remembering her own ordeal, and her sister put a hand to her arm, squeezing it.

'But don't worry. I now know why he had to spell

it out. Because, my dear sister, it seems the man is impotent.'

'So why did he say those things? Why did he take you?'

She shrugged. 'I think he knew there was nothing he could do to challenge the ascension but he still wanted to frustrate things. I'm sure he was hoping the coronation would be delayed. As it was, apparently the news didn't make it to the palace in time.'

She patted the back of Aisha's hand where the remnants of the henna tattoos were still just visible. 'Which reminds me, you are a queen now, and a married woman! Congratulations. Zoltan is such a wonderful man. You must be so happy.'

She shook her head. 'No. Please don't,' she said, pressing her lips together, tears once more springing to her eyes, but this time not from joy.

'Why? What's wrong?'

'It's off. I left him. I don't know if he'll want me back.'

'What?'

She shrugged. 'I left him.'

'How could you do that? Didn't he rescue you from Mustafa?'

Aisha could sit no longer. She jumped up and walked slowly to the window to where the sandy coastline of Al-Jirad appeared as a thick white line in the distance, all the while trying to make sense of all her actions, trying to remember why leaving him was so necessary. 'That was only so he could become king. Everything he's done, it was to become king. That's all he wanted. He didn't really want a wife. He told me that. And he didn't want me.' She spun around, clutching her hands together. 'And, before you say anything, it's been two days now since I left his palace and he hasn't bothered to so much as contact me. So, you see, he doesn't care.

'I will contact him, though,' she said, before scraping her bottom lip with her teeth. 'I've decided to try to make it work, if he wants to try.'

Her sister's eyes opened wide. 'You have no idea, do you? Nobody told you.'

'Told me what?'

'That Zoltan couldn't call you because he was too busy rescuing me.'

'What?'

'It's true. How do you think I got away if not for Zoltan and his friends?' She looked up at the ceiling and blew out a breath. 'Bahir included, as it turns out. Seeing him again was a blast from the past, I can tell you.'

'You know Bahir?' she said, distracted.

It was her sister's turn to shrug, as a strange bleakness filled her eyes. 'It was a long time ago. I'm not sure he wants to remember it either.' She blinked and smiled. 'But that's not the point right now.' She uncurled her long legs from underneath her and padded to where her sister stood. Aisha was still shocked from the revelation that Zoltan had been busy rescuing her sister all the time she'd been thinking he had written her off; still trying to work out why he had done that when there was no risk to his reign. He hated Mustafa, it was true, but why would he risk everything to rescue her sister? Unless...

A tiny and no doubt futile glimmer of hope sparked into life. Unless he had done it somehow for her. But no; he didn't want her.

'The thing is, dear sister,' Marina said, taking her hands in hers, 'what are you going to do now?'

'I don't know,' she said, her heart racing, trying to assimilate and understand everything her sister had told her about Zoltan, everything that made no sense, except that it was Zoltan, and in a way it did. Who else had a grudge against Mustafa and felt he had to prove himself at every turn? Who else would delight in humiliating him further? 'I was going to get in touch anyway.'

'Well, maybe you'll get your chance in a few minutes.'

Realisation skittered down her spine in a tingling rush. 'He's here?'

'He said he wanted to freshen up before he saw you. He said he smells of horse.'

'I like the way he smells,' she mused out loud.

Her sister smiled. 'Maybe you could start by telling him that.'

'My father told me I'd find you here.'

They were in the library, all four of them, freshly showered and looking dangerously dark and sexy. And one of them looked darker and sexier than all the others as he perched on the edge of a desk. He watched her, with those impenetrable dark eyes, his jaw clamped shut, his expression closed.

One by one the other men peeled away, Bahir slapping him on the back, Kadar on the shoulder. Rashid uttered a quick, 'Later,' and with a bow of their heads in her direction they were gone.

He stood and bowed his own head. 'Princess,' he said. 'Queen.'

She looked up at him, at this man she had once had and lost, at the dark planes and sharp angles of his face, and wondered how she could ever have thought he wasn't the most handsome man on the planet. How had she missed such an obvious fact? She wished she could have flung herself into his arms, as she had done with Marina. But if he rejected her, if he pushed her away, she would die.

'I came to thank you. For rescuing Marina.'

'Your sister is well?'

She nodded. 'Very well, and very grateful. We all are.' She searched for something else to say, something to broach the veritable abyss that seemed to stretch between them. And then, because she needed to know if the tiny spark in her heart would be fanned into life or would quickly be extinguished, she went on. 'Why did you do it and not leave it to someone else? Why did you risk yourself on such a rescue now that you are king?'

He dragged in a breath. 'I should never have left Mustafa free to continue to make trouble, after what he had attempted with you. He is the worst kind of opportunist. He saw an opportunity when King Hamra's entire family was wiped out and he kidnapped you to try to steal the crown.'

She frowned. 'You don't think he—?' She stopped. It was too ugly a thought to entertain, too horrible, even for someone like him.

'Do I think he was behind the crash from the start?' He shook his head. 'No. I wondered that once too, but no. Mustafa is a bully, he always has been. But even he would not be capable of murdering so many of his own family. The early reports from the crash investigators seem to support that it was a tragic accident. So, like I said, he saw the opportunity to seize the throne and he took it by kidnapping you.

'And then when that went wrong he saw the chance to frustrate the coronation by taking your sister hostage. I promise he won't try anything again, not where he is now, but how could I do nothing when I felt responsible for what had happened, for letting him go after what he had done to you?'

'Oh.' She looked at the floor as the tiny spark of hope fizzled out. 'I see.' He felt responsible. But he would. When would she ever learn? When would she stop her silly dreams and hopes getting in the way of reality? 'Well, thank you.'

'And, of course, there was the consideration that Marina is your sister.'

She warily lifted her head. 'Because she is now sister-in-law to the King?'

'More than that. I knew you would be upset. I know how much your sister means to you.'

She blinked up at him, touched beyond words, the beginnings of a tentative smile forming on her lips, the spike of tears behind her eyes. 'I'm sorry,' she said, and then wondered why she'd said that when she'd been intending to thank him again. And then she realised it didn't matter if he rejected her apology out of hand and never wanted to see her again—she owed him this apology. 'I'm so sorry for causing you so much trouble.'

'It was Mustafa—'

'No—for being such a spoilt princess. I'm sorry for leaving you the way I did. My father tried to talk sense into me but I wouldn't listen. I thought you didn't care that I'd gone, but all that time you were out there finding my sister.'

She squeezed her eyes shut and put her hands over her face, feeling the dampness on her cheeks from the tears that would be contained no longer. 'I'm such a fool.'

She felt his arms close around her, felt herself pulled

against his chest, and the sheer joy of it brought forth a fresh burst of tears.

'Aisha,' he said, stroking her hair, pressing his lips to it.

She lifted her tear-streaked face, blinking away the moisture in her eyes, and he swept the hair from her face with his fingers. 'You're not still angry with me?' she asked.

He shook his head, the corners of his mouth turned up the slightest fraction. 'It's me who should be asking that. I have treated you appallingly. I was so angry and so resentful with being forced into this position, that I took it out on you. And I understand why you were so hurt the night of the coronation. I'd betrayed your trust once again. And I was going to follow you and tell you that you were right that same night, even though I knew you wouldn't believe me, and tell you that I cared for you.

'And then came the news that Marina had been taken. Hamzah was against me going. But I thought, *I hoped*, that if I could help reunite you with your sister you might understand, just a little, how much you mean to me.'

Her heart swelled in her chest. 'I still can't believe you did that, that you risked everything.'

'But none of it matters, does it?' he said. 'If you can't have what you truly want.'

'What do you truly want?'

He looked down at her with his dark, potent eyes. 'I want you. I want all of you. I want you to be my queen. I want your body. I want your soul. I want you for ever.'

She gasped as he pressed his lips to her forehead before pulling back and she hungered for more of his kiss. 'And I know I fall short of the kind of man you wanted to marry. I know this has all happened the wrong way around and that you have every right to hate me for ever. So I am offering you a choice.'

'What choice?'

He dipped his mouth, kissed the tip of her nose, and she drank in his air and the very essence of him while her lips searched in vain for his.

'You can walk away from our marriage and all that it entails, or you can stay and settle for my flaws and imperfections and, ultimately, my love.'

Her swelling heart sang. 'What did you say?'

'I said I'm giving you a choice.'

'No, not that bit. The other bit.'

'About walking away?'

'No!'

He smiled and kissed her eyes, first one and then the other, but when she angled her face higher, to give him access to her hungry mouth, he withdrew. 'The other choice is my love. You see, I have nothing to offer you, Aisha, that you cannot find in a million other more worthy men, nothing but the one thing only I can give you—my love, if you will accept it.'

'You never told me. I never knew.'

'I didn't know it myself. Not really, not until you walked away and left my heart in pieces on the floor. I love you, Aisha. And I know I am so unworthy. I know I am the last person who deserves it. But will you come back and be my wife? Will you let me love you? Will you find it in your heart to love me one day, even just a little?'

'Oh, Zoltan, yes—a thousand times yes. I love you so much. And now...'

'Now?'

'Now will you kiss me at last?'

He laughed, a low, delicious rumble that vibrated through her all the way to her bones. 'Only a kiss, Aisha, my queen?'

'Don't tell me—you are giving me another choice already?'

His hands scooped down her back to cup her behind, bringing her into even closer contact with the evidence of his desire. 'Only if you want it.'

She smiled up at him, her blood fizzing in anticipation, dizzy with love. 'Oh, I want it, Zoltan. I want it all.'

As his head dipped and his lips brushed against hers with that first delicious contact, she heard him say, 'Then you shall have it.'

And she knew, in her heart, mind and soul, that she already did.

* * * * *

COMING NEXT MONTH from Harlequin Presents®
AVAILABLE SEPTEMBER 18, 2012

#3089 NOT JUST THE GREEK'S WIFE
Lucy Monroe
When Chloe finds herself needing her ex-husband's help,
is she ready to pay his wicked price? Sharing Ariston's
bed, and providing his heir?

#3090 PRINCESS FROM THE SHADOWS
The Santina Crown
Maisey Yates
When Carlotta Santina comes to Prince Rodriguez's
palace as his not-so-blushing bride she brings along a
shameful secret!

#3091 HEIRESS BEHIND THE HEADLINES
Scandal in the Spotlight
Caitlin Crews
Tabloid-hounded Larissa escapes to an island where she
finds herself face-to-face with Jack—the source of her
scandalous reputation!

#3092 THE LEGEND OF DE MARCO
Abby Green
Breaking in to Rocco's office maybe wasn't Gracie's best
idea—now the handsome tycoon won't let her out of his
sight!

#3093 THE SHEIKH'S LAST GAMBLE
Desert Brothers
Trish Morey
Claiming his heir is a risk Bahir has to take, but getting his
ex-lover back will be his biggest gamble yet!

#3094 THE DARKEST OF SECRETS
The Power of Redemption
Kate Hewitt
Grace is helpless to resist Khalis's slow, determined
seduction. But will she risk everything she has for a night
in his bed?

HPCNM0912

REQUEST YOUR FREE BOOKS!

◆ Harlequin *Presents*

PASSION GUARANTEED SEDUCTION

2 FREE NOVELS PLUS
2 FREE GIFTS!

YES! Please send me 2 FREE Harlequin Presents® novels and my 2 FREE gifts (gifts are worth about $10). After receiving them, if I don't wish to receive any more books, I can return the shipping statement marked "cancel." If I don't cancel, I will receive 6 brand-new novels every month and be billed just $4.30 per book in the U.S. or $4.99 per book in Canada. That's a saving of at least 14% off the cover price! It's quite a bargain! Shipping and handling is just 50¢ per book in the U.S. and 75¢ per book in Canada.* I understand that accepting the 2 free books and gifts places me under no obligation to buy anything. I can always return a shipment and cancel at any time. Even if I never buy another book, the two free books and gifts are mine to keep forever.

106/306 HDN FERQ

Name	(PLEASE PRINT)	
Address		Apt. #
City	State/Prov.	Zip/Postal Code

Signature (if under 18, a parent or guardian must sign)

Mail to the **Reader Service:**
IN U.S.A.: P.O. Box 1867, Buffalo, NY 14240-1867
IN CANADA: P.O. Box 609, Fort Erie, Ontario L2A 5X3

Not valid for current subscribers to Harlequin Presents books.

**Are you a current subscriber to Harlequin Presents books
and want to receive the larger-print edition?
Call 1-800-873-8635 or visit www.ReaderService.com.**

* Terms and prices subject to change without notice. Prices do not include applicable taxes. Sales tax applicable in N.Y. Canadian residents will be charged applicable taxes. Offer not valid in Quebec. This offer is limited to one order per household. All orders subject to credit approval. Credit or debit balances in a customer's account(s) may be offset by any other outstanding balance owed by or to the customer. Please allow 4 to 6 weeks for delivery. Offer available while quantities last.

Your Privacy—The Reader Service is committed to protecting your privacy. Our Privacy Policy is available online at www.ReaderService.com or upon request from the Reader Service.

We make a portion of our mailing list available to reputable third parties that offer products we believe may interest you. If you prefer that we not exchange your name with third parties, or if you wish to clarify or modify your communication preferences, please visit us at www.ReaderService.com/consumerschoice or write to us at Reader Service Preference Service, P.O. Box 9062, Buffalo, NY 14269. Include your complete name and address.

HP11B

HARLEQUIN *Romance*

At their grandmother's request, three estranged
sisters return home for Christmas to the small town
of Beckett's Run. Little do they know that this family
reunion will reveal long-buried secrets...
and new-found love.

Discover the magic of Christmas in a brand-new
Harlequin® Romance miniseries.

In October 2012, find yourself
SNOWBOUND IN THE EARL'S CASTLE
by **Fiona Harper**

Be enchanted in November 2012 by a
SLEIGH RIDE WITH THE RANCHER
by **Donna Alward**

And be mesmerized in December 2012 by
MISTLETOE KISSES WITH THE BILLIONAIRE
by **Shirley Jump**

Available wherever books are sold.

*Sensational author Kate Hewitt brings you
a sneak-peek excerpt from THE DARKEST OF SECRETS,
the intensely powerful first story
in her new Harlequin® Presents® miniseries,*
THE POWER OF REDEMPTION.

* * *

"YOU'RE attracted to me, Grace."

"It doesn't matter."

"Do you still not trust me?" he asked quietly. "Is that it? Are you afraid—of me?"

"I'm not afraid of you," she said, and meant it. She might not trust him, but she didn't fear him. She simply didn't want to let him have the kind of power opening your body or heart to someone would give. And then of course there were so many reasons not to get involved.

"What, then?" She just shook her head. "I know you've been hurt," he said quietly and she let out a sad little laugh. He was painting his own picture of her, she knew then, a happy little painting like one a child might make. Too bad he had the wrong paint box.

"And how do you know that?" she asked.

"It's evident in everything you do and say—"

"No, it isn't." She *had* been hurt, but not the way he thought. She'd never been an innocent victim, as much as she wished things could be that simple. And she knew, to her own shame and weakness, that she wouldn't say anything. She didn't want him to look at her differently. With judgment rather than compassion, scorn instead of sympathy.

"Why can't you get involved, then, Grace?" Khalis asked. "It was just a kiss, after all." He'd moved to block the door-

HPEX1012R

way, even though Grace hadn't yet attempted to leave. His face looked harsh now, all hard angles and narrowed eyes, even though his body remained relaxed. A man of contradictions—or was it simply deception? Which was the real man, Grace wondered, the smiling man who'd rubbed her feet so gently, or the angry son who refused to grieve for the family he'd just lost? Or was he both, showing one face to the world and hiding another, just as she was?

Khalis Tannous has ruthlessly eradicated every hint of corruption and scandal from his life. But the shadows haunting the eyes of his most recent—most beautiful— employee aren't enough to dampen his desire. Grace can foresee the cost of giving in to temptation, but will she risk everything she has for a night in his bed?

Find out on September 18, 2012, wherever books are sold!